FOOTPRINTS

OF A NEW YORK CITY

GIRL

By

Amanda McAdams

FOOTPRINTS OF A NEW YORK CITY GIRL

ISBN (979-8-9855173-9-2)

Contents

Contents

CHAPTER 1
BIG CITY GIRL

It was a warm early morning in June of 2010, and the sun was shining brightly while I was sitting at the Pittsburgh International Airport. So many thoughts were going through my head. This was the day I picked up my whole life and decided to move to New York City. My emotions were full of pure thrill and excitement, but I was also anxious and nervous. I have always been an over thinker, so it was pretty normal for me to sit there and let my mind run wild with fictional scenarios.

Pittsburgh has been home to me since I was born. I had known this place forever. It was no doubt a great deal for me to change my entire life and move to another city. But I'll be lying if I said I was not afraid at all, because, at the same time, I was quite scared. My parents were not as excited as I was. They were concerned that I was leaving home and moving to New York City with only a suitcase and very little cash. And as parents, it was normal for them to feel all those emotions, especially when their child is going to move to another city.

I wasn't sure if moving to a new city was really my dream or not, but I knew I wanted more excitement in my life. As a little girl, I always wanted to be the center of attention and do things people would notice. I didn't get much attention when I was little, so I really strived for it in my adult years. I wanted to think outside the box but growing up in Pittsburgh, you didn't do that much. I always wanted to move out and go somewhere, but I was unsure where. I had been putting my passion on the back burner for too long, and I felt like my life was just stuck on autopilot. I knew that moving to a new city would shake up things and open new opportunities for me. I knew that I would never regret this decision.

New York City was never a city I thought I would move to. I had been there once before, but to me, it seemed like a place you only visit for the purpose of sightseeing and touring and not living. Like it was untouchable and only a place for celebrities and very rich people. I knew it would be a gateway to my dreams and passions. I was moving there because I was offered a receptionist position at an investment bank in Manhattan. That was not only appealing but also quite exciting for a small-town girl like me! So, I accepted the offer immediately, sold everything I owned, and went off. I also felt like it would be a new start for me as I had recently broken up with my boyfriend, with whom I was with for five years. This man was my first true love, and I adored everything about him. He was very intriguing and had a Jude Law exuberance about him. He was my everything for a long time, but we couldn't make it work. So, escaping to New York City was a good idea for me.

Luckily, I had a good friend Sarah already living in New York City. I met her a few months prior through her brother, who was one of my good friends. She was going to let me stay at her apartment until I could get on my feet, which I was so grateful for. Her apartment was also very close to where I would be working, so it was another relief that I wouldn't have to worry about the commute. Honestly, I didn't know the first thing about renting an apartment and couldn't afford a place, so the overall situation was working out simply great for me.

As I boarded the flight, I got a bit teary-eyed. Although it wasn't my first flight, I would still say the experience depends on how well you prepare yourself. It was a bittersweet feeling to leave my hometown, family, and friends and just start over in a new place. I have never been alone in my life. I always had friends or family around me, and I never really left Pittsburgh other than the random vacation, which was only to the Jersey shore. I never left home, I never went to a faraway college or lived in a dorm, I never went to a sleep-away camp, nothing. I was always home. So, moving to New York City alone was a huge deal for me. I was very nervous, but I knew I must do this. I was ready to do anything I could to make this work for myself.

After a very short flight, I landed at LaGuardia. It is true that during and after traveling, you feel very different emotions. However, as I landed at the airport, my nerves started sinking as I moved toward this new journey in my life.

I went down to baggage claim, and a nice gentleman asked me, "Do you need a ride into the city?" I responded almost too quickly with, "Yes, please."

I put all my luggage in the car, and just like that, I was headed to Manhattan to start my new journey.

As the driver drove around the city, I looked at the city's beauty. It was even more beautiful than the last time I saw it. New York City had always been a different kind of beauty for me. This time, I saw its beauty as the beauty of people's hard work and struggles for some reason. So, I decided to close my eyes and go deep inside myself, so I could sense the smells, see the sights in my head, and hear the city sounds.

Suddenly, the car stopped, which disrupted my daydreaming. The driver looked back at me and said, "The total is $175."

As you can imagine, I was shocked by the ride's price; to be honest, paying that much wasn't really in my first week's budget. With a sigh, I handed him the cash and got out. I went straight to the doorman. He was a lovely, older gentleman who had been working there for years. The doorman walked me to Sarah's apartment because she was at work. As I was escorted to her apartment, many thoughts were racing through my head,

"What will her place look like? Will there be enough space for both of us?"

I opened the door with a bit of a shock. It was so small. I had never seen an apartment like this in my life. I later found out that it was the average standard apartment in New York City. It was about 400 square feet with a tiny kitchen, two closets, a couch, and a bed. I had no idea how we would survive in this tiny place. I took a two-minute tour, dropped my bags, and called Sarah.

"Hey girl, how're you doing?" I said as soon as Sarah picked up my call.

"Hi, babe! I'm good, and you? How was the flight?" she replied.

Before I could even respond, she told me to come to her office on fourteenth between sixth and seventh and hung up the phone. Now I had no idea what fourteenth between sixth and seventh meant. I knew I was not ready for the subway, and Uber didn't exist then. So, I freshened up a bit, walked outside, and stood on the corner waving a cab down. One pulled up instantly. I just got in and said fourteenth between sixth and seventh, and off we went. I felt a small sense of pride when I got in that cab and directed the cab driver in the right direction. Cabs barely existed in Pittsburgh, so I decided to just hop in and pretend I was a real New Yorker. It was exciting!

I arrived at Sarah's office. She worked for a production company. I texted her that I had arrived. She replied, telling me to check in with the receptionist. So, I got off the elevator and checked in with the receptionist, just like Sarah told me to. The receptionist looked in my direction with zero interest or acknowledging that I was standing in front of her. I told her I was meeting Sarah, and she still seemed like she didn't care. It was a very cool office space inside a big loft. Everyone was in jeans which to me was cool.

There were a few offices, but most people were just on their laptops. Someone was in the kitchen, someone on the couch in the reception area, someone in a conference room, and there was a cool playlist on as well. While the receptionist and I just stared at each other in silence, Sarah came around the corner.

"Welcome to New York City," yelled Sarah as she hugged me.

I felt butterflies in my stomach hearing this. We sat and had a good chat for a bit. She had about an hour left at work, so I decided to respond to all the messages I received from everyone back home.

It was now the end of the workday and happy hour with Sarah was my next adventure. We went to a nice lounge by her office, and I was mesmerized by the décor, drinks, and food. I had never been in such a cool place where the energy was so overwhelming. I met a few of her friends at happy hour. Most were very nice, but a few looked at me like, "this poor girl doesn't have a clue."

They were extremely good looking and well dressed, so I felt out of place. I never had expensive clothes growing up. I belonged to a very middle-class family. My parents worked hard to give me what I needed, but I wasn't the girl walking around in Gucci. They didn't bother me, and we had such a great time. We stayed there for a good bit, then went to Tribeca for a late dinner.

When we got to the restaurant, I was blown away by its beauty. It was this gorgeous underground low-lit wide-open space with a lovely long table for us to have dinner. Now, this was way out of my budget, but Sarah offered to pay for me since it was my first night out. After that, more of her friends arrived for dinner, and she ended up sitting me next to a guy named Nate. Of course, he was a very good-looking man and had that New York swag. The whole night was like I was living in a movie. The energy of the place and the people were very different. After dinner, I thought we would go home, but Sarah had other plans. We went to a dance club until after midnight. Once again, it was a cool underground club by Sarah's office. Nate joined us, and he and I were getting along well, and after multiple martini's, we got flirty. We danced for hours, and at one point, the next thing I knew, Nate was kissing me in the corner.

Shocked? Yes!

I didn't really know what to do after that, and he just looked at me and said, "I hope I can see you again."

I walked back to the girls and told them about what had just happened. They all rolled their eyes and said, "He always does that."

I didn't really think much into it, to be honest. I just wanted to have the best time that night as I knew that come Monday, I had to start my job.

The weekend came and went, and I barely slept Sunday night because I was so nervous about Monday. Sarah and I were getting ready for work in her little studio apartment that morning. She had been living in the city for quite a long time, and I was fascinated by her. She was very well put together. She had a great energy that I enjoyed. I started to go through my bag for something to wear.

"Babe, how's this dress for work today?" I asked Sarah while showing her my outfit.

"No! Don't wear that. Come here. You can borrow something out of my closet," Sarah replied.

She was very nice to let me borrow some of her clothes for work until I could get my paycheck and do some shopping. I was short of cash and could barely get anything for myself, so I was very grateful to have her helping me. I noticed, though, that between the girls I met and Sarah, everyone constantly wore black. Sarah's closet was filled with everything black, but I didn't have anything black. I always loved dressing in various colors, so I didn't really understand the black clothes vibe.

I made my way to my new office in the black dress Sarah let me borrow. It was on the thirty-second floor of a big skyscraper. I walked out to the lobby, and there were two big glass doors to a mesmerizing office setting. My boss came out to greet me and welcome me. I was introduced to everyone there. Everyone was so lovely and welcoming. I had a gorgeous desk up front, and it felt like I would enjoy it. I don't want to bore you with all the details of my responsibilities, but I felt that this was going to be a good fit for me.

The day quickly went by as I was busy. I walked home feeling so good about myself. It was as if I was on cloud nine and couldn't be stopped. Sarah and I met for dinner, and I told her all about my day. She was so excited for me. I felt grateful to have Sarah by my side during the start of my journey.

My next week at work went great; the people I worked with were cordial and friendly. The company was a boutique firm, so there were not many bankers, but we started to become a small family. This made me feel comfortable since I did not know many people at that time. I was happy with how everything was going. I would call my mom daily to check in and would tell her that things were going well, and I felt like this could be a great place for me. She still wasn't quite on board with all of it, but she was happy that I was happy.

I have always been the person who does everything for everyone. But finally, this was a chance for me to be happy and do something for myself. I had started settling down in the city, and it took me a few weeks, until everything started feeling normal. However, I had done nothing besides go to work and follow Sarah everywhere. One usual night Sarah and I were watching TV.

"We need to get on the train for dinner," Sarah told me while getting up from the couch and going towards her closet.

"Oh, we are going somewhere far on a train. Sounds fun," I replied with an exciting tone.

"We are going on the subway," uttered Sarah while rolling her eyes at me.

She knew many people here, which was very helpful for me. All the places we went to were just amazing. In short, I was obsessed with the city. I finally received my first paycheck. It gave me a taste of what was in store. Now I could easily start searching for a place and pay my bills. I could buy myself some nicer clothes and give Sarah some money for everything she has done for me.

I was excited to look for a place of my own. I reached out to one of my friends in Pittsburgh, who now lived in New York City, to see if he knew anyone looking for a roommate. He told me he had two guy friends who lived in Brooklyn and needed a roommate. He sent me their information and I ended up contacting one of them on Facebook messenger. The Guy's name was Josh, and we set up a time for me to see the apartment. He told me to take the F train to Church

Avenue. I had no idea what he was talking about but knew I had to start figuring out the subway system.

I googled what train to take and went to Brooklyn the next day. It was a forty-five minute train ride from my office. I got off at Church Avenue, looked around, and thought, "Okay, this is Brooklyn."

The apartment was close to the subway, so I didn't have to walk far. It was a lovely brownstone on the corner of the street.

I knocked at the door, and Josh answered. I was a bit taken back as he was a good-looking guy with a Bradley Cooper vibe and a ton of tattoos. He showed me around the apartment and the room I would have. The apartment was very big and had enough space for three people. He told me it was $800 per month, and I immediately said, "I'll take it." I gave them the first month's rent and security and moved in that weekend.

I felt happy with everything. Work was going well, and I also had this great apartment with two roommates I liked. I was really shocked at how everything was working out and felt a little bit of relief and a feeling of pride once again, just like when I was in the cab. People always say moving anywhere is not easy, but New York City is especially hard, so I felt proud of myself.

That Wednesday, I was at work, and Nate messaged me, just checking in on me and how it had been going. He was born and raised in New York City, which I thought was very intriguing. He asked if I would meet him for drinks after work. At this point, the only people I had been around were Sarah and my roommates. I was a bit weary from what the girls said at happy hour, but I said yes anyway. He asked if I could meet him at his apartment on Park Avenue, and we would then walk somewhere for drinks. I finished up my day and headed over. I stopped at the entrance of the building with my jaw dropped to the ground.

The building was beautiful, very old school, and charming. Everyone that was walking out was dripping in Gucci, Chanel, and Louis Vuitton. In my head, it didn't make sense that he lived there. He buzzed me up to his apartment, which was utterly insane. It was right out of a magazine. He went on to tell me that it was his mom's apartment, which made more sense.

He offered me a drink, to which my response was, "I thought we were going out."

"Let's stay here instead," he said.

I started to feel extremely uncomfortable, and he was starting to get a little bit too flirty. I looked at him and said I couldn't stay, and I walked out. I got down on the sidewalk and now realized what the girls meant about Nate.

It was finally Friday, and it was my birthday weekend. I have always been so enamored with my birthday. I will celebrate it for a month - such a Leo characteristic. I didn't have many friends in the city and didn't really have the money to plan a big birthday party for myself, so Sarah and my roommates had set up drinks at a cool spot in Brooklyn for that night, and I was really looking forward to having a nice birthday. It was a typical day until my boss asked me into the conference room. Nothing was on my mind, so I walked straight to the conference room, where he asked me to sit down.

"Amanda, I am so sorry. Unfortunately, we will have to let you go due to budget restrictions," he said in a sympathetic tone.

My stomach went immediately into my throat. Tears started to well up in my eyes. I kept asking him why and he just kept saying he was sorry. He told me if anything opened back up, he would call me.

After his sixth sorry, I became distraught and walked out of the room. I packed up my desk and left the building. It was the middle of the afternoon, and I had a key to Sarah's apartment, so I just went there.

I had lost not only my job, but I felt like such a failure in such a short period of time. I have always been such a hard worker, and never in my life have I been let go from a job. I understood what he was saying to me, but I didn't. I thought I did something wrong to deserve this, and that feeling took over my whole being. I couldn't stop the thousands of thoughts that started striking my mind.

"How am I supposed to pay my rent? Should I move back to Pittsburgh? How am I going to manage my expenses?"

I was getting very worked up as I walked down 2nd avenue to Sarah's apartment. I was crying, and the one thing I did notice was that no one stopped or even looked at me. I felt so alone at that very moment in a city of millions. I didn't know who to call first or if I should even tell anyone. I walked into Sarah's building, and her doorman looked at me with a questioning thought of, "shouldn't you be at work?" I just kept my head down and walked by. I didn't want him to see me crying.

I walked into the apartment and just sat on the couch crying. Finding yourself out of work makes you question yourself and question what you will do going forward. I had to talk to someone and I knew that at least I had Sarah to talk about what was happening. I didn't want to tell my roommates as I didn't want them to think I couldn't pay rent, and then they would kick me out. I wasn't on the lease, so I thought they could do whatever they wanted. My mind couldn't stop racing. I didn't know what I would do or how to navigate through this.

CHAPTER 2
WORK HARD, PLAY HARD

As I sat on Sarah's bed feeling sorry for myself, I decided I needed to call her. I told her what happened with trembling lips, and much to my surprise, she didn't think it was a big deal.

After hearing me out, she said, "Just go out and look for a job."

Like it was just so easy. I was so shocked by her response. I was already shattered into pieces, and her response disappointed me. I wanted someone to feel bad for me and have the same negative thoughts. I knew deep down that I needed to get motivated, but it was just hard getting to that place mentally.

My head was spinning around, and my nerves continuously sent me these weird signals, which put me in a bad space physically. When I get nervous or anxious, I stop eating, which I knew would also happen this time. I didn't want to go home. I didn't want people to think I was a failure. I needed to figure out something quick as my last paycheck was running low, and I now had bills to pay. It was making me feel uneasy, and my ego was taking over my thoughts. I had no clue where even to start. I just wanted to sit there and feel bad for myself.

I ended up staying at Sarah's a few nights. I was clearly not used to facing such problems in my life. Sarah told me not to worry about it and to look for another job. She was behaving so casually about it, whereas I was losing my mind over it. However, she calmed me down, so I could try to focus on my next steps.

Life does not always play out the way we want it to since situations are beyond our control and cannot always be manipulated. Sometimes, the things we want in our lives are not meant for us. I had to stop giving myself unrealistic expectations that would only cause me to be more upset. I had to go easy and realize that I would get there eventually.

I went back to my place and started hunting for jobs. In the meantime, I was texting Sarah back and forth. She suggested that I get a bartending job. I had little to no experience in bartending, so I was annoyed that she was telling me that. Sarah told me to stop making excuses and just make up a resume and drop it off at bars. I took her advice finally and created a bartending resume.

That Monday, I went into the city like I was going to work. I knew I had to drop off my resume to so many places. I walked so much that day from the Upper East Side to Union Square.

Finally, my last stop was at an Irish pub that was located off the beaten path in Irving Place. I walked in and found the manager, Connor, behind the bar. I walked up to him and asked if they were hiring.

"I can take your resume and give you a call if we have an opening," he replied to me.

I handed my resume to him and went to Sarah's office to meet her. I was still not feeling any better as my life felt chaotic and all over the place. Everything seemed so difficult and pointless. My 'low' moods were lasting longer than usual, and I could not 'shake it.' I had no interest in doing anything, and I was not taking care of myself physically either.

I was temporarily frustrated with my actions and behaviors. Sarah told me that this was my own way of processing my feeling of disappointment. But she had some good news for me as well. She had talked to her boss, and they were going to let me do some data entry for them.

Oh, thank God! I thought maybe too loud that I doubted Sarah could hear my thoughts a little.

I enjoyed their office environment and knowing I had somewhere to go every day was very helpful. I grew up in a structured household, so in my adult life, I felt more comfortable and motivated to get things done when I had a routine.

The next day, I woke up early to go to Sarah's office. Until around 10:00 AM, there wasn't a soul in the place, allowing me to search for employment online. My main problem was that I had no prior experience in New York City. I wanted to stay in the finance profession since I thought it was the most lucrative, but I only had three weeks of experience. So, I was just going with the flow. The morning went fast, and that afternoon, I received a call. It was Connor from the Irish Pub. He quickly said, "We will hire you as a waitress. You start tomorrow."

I went to Sarah yelling and shouting that I got a job. I was acting as if I had never received a call for a job or as if

I had never been hired before in my life. Everyone in the office glanced at me like, "Okay, small-town girl, relax."

Knowing I had another job made me feel a lot better since I believed that I could at least pay my rent if I had two jobs. I felt like a small weight was lifted off my shoulders.

I had to tell the boys what was going on at this point because now I would be working nights. I decided to finally talk to them and let them know about everything, so we sat down in our living room, and I told them what was going on in my life for quite a few days.

They both looked at me and said, "Amanda, this happens all the time. You will be fine."

I was relieved knowing that they were fine with that. They were quite supportive as well. I didn't know them that well, so I wasn't sure what the response was going to be.

It was finally the first evening working at the pub. I made sure I got there a little bit early. I walked in and was greeted by Connor and his dad, Pat, who was the actual owner of the pub.

Pat had an Irish brogue which I was immediately intrigued by. I have never been around someone with an accent, so I enjoyed it when he spoke, I couldn't understand what he was saying, but I happily listened. It was a charming pub, very Irish and old-fashioned. They had antique cash registers behind the bar, and the décor was very Irish. Connor paired me with a long-serving waiter at the restaurant. His name was Jose. He took some time to show me what my responsibilities would be as a waitress. He was a very funny guy, which made me feel comfortable working with him. Connor informed me that day shift bartenders work until 6:30 PM, after which the night shift takes over.

However, the one-night shift bartender was in early that night. His name was Paul. He was also Irish but a smaller skinny guy—a feisty guy. Seemed like he was one to get in a lot of fights but would also give you the shirt off his back. I didn't pay much attention to him and just listened as he told me where things were behind the bar.

It was now 6:30 PM, and I was working behind the bar, figuring out what was going on for the time being. Finally, the door swung open, and he walked in. When I looked up, this guy caught my eye for some reason. It was as if I had known him for years or something. You could tell he had a chip on his shoulder and a cool vibe about him. He sported a massive head of curly hair and big headphones. He appeared more like a regular at the pub, but then he headed downstairs, where the employees' personal belongings were kept. I didn't inquire who he was and returned to my business. He came upstairs in his black shirt and pants and walked right in my direction.

"Hi, my name's Niall. Like the river." Said Niall in his cute Irish accent.

I was a little taken aback when he made a reference to the Nile River before I could even say my name. But, hey, I was not the one to pass judgment. I introduced myself, and we began a little conversation about where I was from. It seemed we had arrived in New York City roughly at the same time. He gave me a nod and jumped behind the bar alongside Paul.

The night flew quickly, and Niall made it extremely enjoyable for me. He was well-known among the regulars. I finished around midnight. I was happy with my shift, the environment of the pub, and the people I had just met. Then came the tough part: taking the train back to Brooklyn.

At this point, I had only been on the subway a handful of times with Sarah or Josh, so I really had absolutely no clue what I was doing. All I knew was the F train was near my apartment, so I had to get there. Luckily, there was an F train by the pub. I was a bit scared walking down the steps to the subway as I was alone, and it was late. When I stepped into the subway car, there were a few people, so I didn't feel too scared. I noticed a guy across from me who was really drunk. I decided not to pay any attention to him. I put my headphones on and kept my head down. I was far into Brooklyn, so there were a lot of stops.

I had about four more stops to go when the drunk guy got up and started stumbling. Again, I didn't look at him. The next thing I knew, he stood in front of me and just threw up on my legs. I was in utter shock. The doors opened, and he walked out. My first subway ride alone, and now I have someone's vomit all over me. A nice lady gave me a few napkins that she had in her purse, and I just sat there for the next four stops with vomit on me. At that exact moment, I questioned why I was living in New York City. I got home safely and went straight into the shower. I threw my clothes away. What a mess!

My new schedule was working out nicely. I'd work for Sarah during the day and then head to the pub for the night shift as a waitress. Niall would come in every night with his Irish swag and work the entire room. He exuded a certain allure. I couldn't put my finger on what it was. Was it his baby blues, his crooked smile, or simply how he interacted with people? I had no clue. He piqued my interest, and I loved watching him bartend since it made my nights go by faster. It seemed like a lot of the people came into the pub just to see Niall. He had that charismatic attitude about him, and people adored it.

I was enjoying my time working in the pub. But unfortunately, I realized I wasn't making enough money. I would pay my rent and barely had anything left for myself. I was surprised that I couldn't seem to make enough money. Waitressing wasn't enough because most customers preferred to go to the bar and drink rather than sit at a table. Helping Sarah also wasn't paying well. Now, I was starting to feel sorry for myself once again. I would have to find a third job to make ends meet. I have felt like my life is all about work, work, and work, lately. It was starting to affect me mentally. I was brought up to be a hard worker, but it gets to you when you are working 24/7.

I began to feel a little panicked at this point, but I paid the rent for that month and continued. The only saving grace was that I could eat for free at the pub, which meant I didn't have to buy groceries as much as I used to. Also, because I was working every day, I didn't go out at this point, which meant that I also didn't have to buy many clothes besides what I wore to Sarah's office and the pub. My uniform at the pub was a black shirt and black pants, so it was a cheap, easy find at H&M. Feeling panicked went on for a while. The only time I was happy was when Niall was at work. I could be in the worst mood, and he would just look at me with his crooked smile and those baby blues and I couldn't help but just smile.

Niall and I became great friends very quickly. He was the only person I had in New York City besides Sarah and my roommates. After a few months, I began interacting with the pub's regulars. There were a handful of regulars that came in for happy hour pretty much every weeknight. Tony was an older gentleman, brilliant and very well dressed. He had been coming there for years and was very kind. Phillip was my age and studying at NYU. He lived close by and would stop at the pub on his way home from class.

They also had a few friends that would come by as well, have a few drinks, and head home. They were very polite, and I really started making friendships with all of them. And Niall and I were labeled as the A-team! Everyone admired us, and the regulars wanted me behind the bar with him, which I thought would be such a great idea. We would have so much fun together, and then I would make good money!

Pat promptly stopped that idea because he didn't want a girl behind the bar at such a late hour. He wasn't being mean when he said this, he really cared about my safety, which I admired. On the other hand, Connor offered me the opportunity to bartend during the day and, if I chose, then be a waitress at night.

I needed a way to supplement my income, and it appeared like bartending was the way to go! So, it's back to the drawing board with a new plan. I told Sarah that I would be doing the day and night shifts at the pub and would no longer be able to work with her. She was fine with that, just if I was happy.

I was working nonstop and barely making ends meet. I thought this new schedule would be more helpful financially, but it wasn't. The pub wasn't a place people went during the day. The area was off the beaten path, so not too many people knew about it or would walk by. Most days, I would be on my own with the cook Leo. He and I grew very close. He was an older gentleman from Jamaica who made me laugh every shift.

I would chat with Niall a lot about how I was feeling. He would always say, "Don't you think everyone would come to New York City if it was easy?"

Every time I was down, he knew how to pick me back up again, which was so heartwarming to me as we had only known each other for a few weeks.

One night, I was walking to the F train and saw a homeless woman on the street with her child. I stopped and gave her a few bucks and then realized I needed to stop feeling sorry for myself. Instead, I should be grateful for my position at the pub, where everyone has become like family to me. Strangers I only met a few weeks ago treated me as if I were their child and would go to any length to help me. They all knew I wasn't making the best money during the day shift. Happy hour started at 5:00 PM, so I had the regulars there at the tail end of my shift and they were always so generous with tips. They were very kind to me. When moving here, I would have never thought that New Yorkers were so kind.

It was finally Sunday. I know many people don't get excited about Sundays, but that was my only day off. It was Niall's day off as well. He planned a brunch that Sunday as he always did. This was just my first one. It was a Cuban place in Alphabet City, which I had no clue what that meant, but I was excited to try new places in the city. Luckily, it was an all-included brunch which was unlimited sangria and your meal for twenty-three dollars. Perfect for my budget. I met him there, and it was him and about five of his mates. We took our seats at one of the biggest tables and just drank and ate until we couldn't anymore. It was such a cool restaurant, and we had the best time. That Sunday, I met Manny. He was one of Niall's good friends with whom he played soccer. He was very smart, witty, and handsome, originally from California. We all got along great as if we knew each other for years. I knew right then and there that Niall and Manny were going to be my friends forever.

Every week I would work my shifts at the pub while Niall and I became closer and closer. There was just something about him. The way we looked at each other, the hugs we gave each other, the jokes we made. It truly was the sweetest friendship I had experienced. I think starting a friendship with no previous connection was the very reason why we were so attached to one another. Back home, most of my friends, who I adored, were schoolmates or children of my parents' friends. I had never formed a friendship with someone I had no prior links to before in my life.

That next weekend Niall's dad was visiting. That was the time when I got introduced to Ray. When I first met him, he reminded me of Santa Claus. This man was a real spitfire, and I enjoyed being around him. Niall and I took a few shifts off that week to spend with his dad, and this man wore us out. That Saturday, I was working the day shift after a week of drinking with those two, and I was totally spent! I knew I wanted to go straight home that day, and then Ray walked in.

"Hey, Pet," he said. "Ready for another go?"

I said no immediately to him, but before I knew it I found myself hanging out with him, Niall, and Manny that night. After spending time with Ray, I realized where Niall got his great personality from. He was just an absolute legend of a guy. He was very sweet as well. The kind of person you just felt at home with.

After that week of partying, I needed a break from it all. I was getting ready to go to the pub one morning and received a voicemail from my landlord. I was behind on my rent once again. My roommates and I paid him the rent separately, so they were never aware if or when I was late on rent. I knew I couldn't go back to my previous state of depression. So, there I was, again, strolling the streets with my resume! This time I geared the resume towards sales. I worked in sales a little bit when I lived in Pittsburgh.

I worked at a radio station back home, and they had an office here in New York City. I contacted my old boss to see if she could set me up with an interview, to which she was happy to help. I had an interview scheduled the week later, but I could just tell I wasn't going to get it. I just didn't have the sales experience in New York City. I tried a few other companies, and they said the same thing. I kept plugging away while I was working at the pub.

One evening my old boss from the radio station called and said that her brother, who was a TV producer, would be in town doing an event and he needed help. It wasn't a full-time job, but they would pay me $500 to help. She told me to call him and sort out the details. I had met her brother Tommy a few times before. He was slightly older than me and seemed like a really great guy. I even had a bit of a crush on him. He asked me to meet him for drinks, and we could talk about the weekend event.

I met up with him that night, and he was just so cute! I had some butterflies; I found it difficult to get any real words out of my mouth. I felt like a teenager who recently developed a crush on someone. We couldn't stop chatting after we had a few shots of tequila. He was hilarious and constantly made me laugh, and I loved every minute of it. He explained the job to me and told me he would see me on Saturday. I went home that night feeling like a giddy schoolgirl and was so excited for Saturday.

The event was held in Central Park. The job was a little tough for me, but it was surely a lot of fun. It was all day, and by the time we were done, we all were exhausted. However, Tommy and I got the energy to go have dinner, which turned into pickle back shots and karaoke until all hours of the night. I loved being around him. He made my soul lighten up with laughter and positivity. I knew we had to leave because I could see the sun coming up through the bar windows. We walked outside, where there was a cab parked. He picked me up and sat me on the hood of the cab and looked directly into my eyes. It all felt so dreamy. I looked back at him, and before I knew it, he gently grabbed my face and started kissing me. Here I was, making out with a guy I liked, on the hood of a cab and just two days ago, I was depressed and hated living in New York City.

We went our separate ways that night, but I knew that night would always be a memorable one for me, and he always said I would be a 'big city girl.'

It was time to go back to real life. I had a week of fun with Niall and had a wonderful time with Tommy, and now I had to start looking for another job because being broke was not going to go away.

I started looking for jobs in the medical field as it was more related to my educational background since I have a degree in that field. At the time, Craigslist was the place to go. I found a post for a medical technologist at an Endocrinologist's office on the Upper West Side. I applied.

A week later, I received a call from her, inviting me to come in for an interview. Because her office was on the Upper West Side and I was still in Brooklyn, I arrived early. It took me roughly an hour to get there. The waiting room was packed when I arrived, so I checked in and waited patiently.

After about thirty minutes, I was called back to meet with the doctor. As soon as I sat down, I had this feeling of being at home or something, and I felt completely at ease in her presence. She was a very well-dressed woman with great energy. She went into the interview process right away. The office manager, who was her husband, was also present there. Every question was nailed in my head. I always knew I had the talent to appear great in interviews, and this interview was no exception. For some reason, I relished being grilled. She said it would be a part-time job, and I'd oversee the lab and phlebotomy.

I was fine with working part-time at first because I was still working at the pub. I felt wonderful after the interview. In any case, I knew I still had the job at the pub, and I could keep looking for other opportunities. After approximately a week, I received a call from the doctor's office, and they told me I got the job! I was overjoyed because I finally had a job worthy of my skills and education. I'd have a consistent salary and health insurance, and I'd be able to work my way up. The only drawback was that this job wasn't paying well enough for me to leave the pub. I was fine with it because I had been I was used to working multiple jobs at a time.

I started working for the doctor a week later and was very excited about it. My first few days involved training and getting to understand everything. I met the receptionist Megan who was quiet, but very sweet. I felt like working there would give me a purpose. I could help people, and I always enjoyed doing that. The doctor was always uplifting and open to all my questions during the training process. She wanted me to succeed. This woman was the type of woman who wanted to help everyone as well. I had this sense that she was going to be a part of my life forever and guide me in the right direction. I was once again back on track!

CHAPTER 3

LOSING PITTSBURGH

By then, I had been working at the doctor's office and the pub for a couple of months. I was going out a lot more, especially with the Doc (which I called her for short) and Megan. We would often go out to have casual yet amazing dinners and brunches on the weekend. She was becoming my New York City Mom, since I didn't have any family around me here. Everything was going according to plan. They showed me so many cool places in New York City that I was falling in love with it more and more each passing day. I hadn't been back home in a while as I could never afford it. I did go back a few times on a bus that only cost me ten dollars. It was an agonizing trip as it was an 11-hour ride on a bus.

Pittsburgh is a town that set a very different image and standard of living in my mind. Living there, I always felt like you had to marry your high school sweetheart, have children, and that would be your forever life. That was, in fact, me at one point. When I was twenty-two years old, I got engaged and started planning a wedding. Naturally, my mom was thrilled since I was following the same path most Pittsburgh girls followed. I, on the other hand, knew something didn't feel right.

I didn't feel the joy of getting married that young. I always wanted more from my life but being with him meant I had to give up on my dreams. It was not like he did not love me; he did love me and built a lovely home for us, but the problem was that he wanted me to stay at home and raise children. That was not me! I had no desire to spend my life like that at age of twenty-two. Everyone was ecstatic that I was getting married. Invitations had been sent, a shower had been held, and the wedding was just three weeks away. Still, I couldn't convince myself to get married to him.

In my head and heart, I knew I couldn't do it, but I had no clue how I was going to tell everyone. I was extremely stressed about it and knew I had to speak up and let someone know how I was feeling. So, I gathered all the courage I had in my body and spoke up to my mom, telling her that I wanted to cancel the wedding. To my surprise, she was very understanding about my wishes and supported my every move. That was one thing I cherished about my mom; she was not only my mom but also my best friend. She always had my back in everything and supported all my decisions.

I don't know why I have this constant need to put people's feelings before mine and never actually focus on myself. However, it was high time I should be thinking about my emotions and keeping them on priority. I needed to do what was right for me. I told my fiancé how I felt about the wedding and how I wanted to cancel it. Listening to me, he got extremely upset, but there was absolutely nothing he could do about it. Nothing worked as planned, but I was glad I was able to take a stand for myself. I knew I wanted a different life, and taking this step gave me a little hope.

I was starting to feel more confident living in New York City, but I knew I had to start making more effort to visit my family. Since my parents only had two children, me, and my brother RJ, I knew they would be excited for me to visit them.

RJ and I were two years apart in age. When I was young, my parents got divorced, and RJ didn't handle it as well as I did. He got himself into a lot of trouble because he hung out with the wrong crowd. It impacted him adversely that caused problems for our family as well.

He was abusing drugs and had been making lots of awful bad choices in life that were not at all healthy by any means and caused him trouble. It was heartbreaking to watch my brother go through the struggles he was dealing with. I felt like there wasn't much I could do to help, because when I did try to help, he would ignore any advice I would give.

Mental health is a real issue for people. We just didn't know what the remedy for it was. We worked hard at trying to make him feel that he was in a better place, but it always seemed like nothing was working. It seemed that he was happy being in a depressed state because that felt a lot easier for him. Seeing RJ in that condition broke my heart and to see my mom and grandmother go through the pain, broke my heart even more. When my parents divorced, my brother and I moved in with my mom, who did anything she could to raise us. I tried my best to help her with everything, but I was only thirteen at the time so couldn't do much.

But after moving to New York City, I couldn't be around them constantly to help them with the situation. RJ kept down the same path, and it angered me. He was not ready to give up on his patterns, which annoyed me greatly. My parents and my grandmother were doing so much to make him feel better, but he constantly hurt them with his actions. I don't do well when others hurt people, and I was giving up on him at that point. Mental health back then wasn't really a thing, so to me, I just thought it was just nonsense. My brother and I never had that brother-sister connection, so for me, it was easier to act aloof. At one point, we stopped talking to each other, and I just continued to try and support my parents and grandmother as much as possible.

I remember it was Thursday, and I was home early from the pub. I would always try my best to come home early from the pub whenever it was possible. It was around 11:00 PM, and I was in bed when my phone rang. I grabbed my phone to see who was calling me and saw it was my mom. I simply declined the call as I was tired and did not feel like talking to her at that time. All I wanted to do at that time was to sleep. However, it rang again, and it was again my mom. It felt kind of weird because she never used to call me that late, and now. I knew she might have something urgent to talk about, so I decided to answer it.

"Hello?" I said as I picked up the call. All I could hear was my mom crying and screaming. "What happened? Why are you crying?" I asked her, panicking.

But she did not respond and kept crying. I suddenly jumped out of my bed due to curiosity and stress.

"Please tell me what's wrong, mom," I asked her again. "RJ is DEAD!!!" She replied to me while crying.

As soon as I heard those words coming from my mom's mouth on the other side of the phone, I felt like my soul had just fallen out of my body. My mind became foggy, and I was unable to think straight. I felt empty within seconds. I wanted to scream and run back home as fast as I could. But instead, I got frozen—unable to talk, walk, or pretty much do anything.

It was so hard for me to think about anything at that moment. I was totally numb to what she said, and she kept repeating herself. She had told me that she had found him dead in his apartment. Once she hung up, I just sat there in the corner of my bed because I had no idea what to do or how to feel. I didn't even cry. I only sat there in utter confusion and shock.

I waited for myself to act normal. Instead, I was in intense shock, and my body only maintained this state for a short period of time. I have seen people who are good at coping with traumatic experiences. I just realized I was not those kinds of people. I needed to understand what was happening to my mind and body. It was a scary experience for me. I did not know how to manage my emotions, so my reaction was more sustained to trauma. I was unconsciously tensing my muscles in my shock state. There was a rapid increase in my heart rate. I didn't believe what I had just heard. I kept asking myself how something so horrific would happen to us. I remained seated on my bed and just stared at the floor in a foggy daze.

But then I understood that I needed to go home and be with my family. Because of rent that week, I only had twenty dollars in my bank account. My roommates had invited friends over for drinks that evening. I walked out to the living room, looking like a zombie. Seeing me in that condition, everyone fell silent and stared at me, concerned. I still wasn't crying, but I somehow managed to tell them what had happened. As hard as it was, I told them my brother was dead. Listening to me, they all stood on their feet instantly and hugged me. I did have to ask Josh for money to get back home, which he was happy to help me with.

Afterward, I went outside and sat on our porch, smoking a cigarette. I dialed Niall's number, and my eyes welled up with tears as soon as I heard Niall's voice. I could not stop asking him why and how all of that had happened. My heart bled with sorrow, especially for my mother. No parent should have to deal with something so cruel, like finding their child dead. I just kept thinking about my parents and grandmother and how they must be feeling so heartbroken.

Niall came over and simply held me in his arms. I wasn't sure how I was feeling. The pain had filled my heart and taken over my entire body. I was unable to feel any other emotion. Once again, I knew I had to put my mother's feelings before mine, as she needed my support in such a horrific time.

Niall stayed with me that night after I took some Nyquil. I got up early and flew back to Pittsburgh on the first flight. The tears were streaming down my face as I sat at the airport that morning, posting about my brother on Facebook. I never thought my trip back home would be for my brother's funeral. When I arrived at my mom's house, she looked at me speechlessly, unable to do anything but stare at me and cry.

I didn't know what to say to her, but I kept my emotions to myself to not cause another reason for her to get upset any further. My grandmother was also there; seeing her cry in agony was heartbreaking. I had to make sure I was in good shape to be able to support them both. My grandmother was a big part of my life, and I absolutely adored her. Seeing her sad and heartbroken, as well as my mom, flooded me with so many painful emotions. Watching them suffer was like getting stabbed in my heart repeatedly.

My parents organized everything, which I know was hard for them. They even had him buried in his favorite Pittsburgh Penguin jersey. He passed at the age of thirty, and there were many people there to show their condolences. I went straight into my business mode and ensured everyone was alright besides myself. I had informed the Doctor and Connor about my situation and had taken a week off from work. They were so understanding and told me I could take as much time as I needed. Although the worst part was that no matter how much time I needed, I could not take it as I was running short on money. I could not believe I had to think about my financial crisis when my brother had just passed away. The week flew by, I was so busy helping my mom that I hardly realized how fast the time was going by.

One night, I was sitting with my stepfather and said, "I think I'll have to move back to Pittsburgh now. I can't leave her to deal with this on her own."

"Don't move back. Just keep doing what you're doing," he said.

I felt that if I returned to New York City, I would be such a terrible daughter. I spoke with my mom about it, and she said she just wanted me to be happy and return to New York City. It took a lot of persuasion before I booked my return flight to New York City. When I arrived home that day, my roommates were there to console me, and I received several cards and flowers.

The next several days were difficult for me since business mode had ended, and I was beginning to feel the effects. However, I had no idea how to handle everything I was feeling and going through. It made me angry, and I didn't know what to do about it. So, after my shift, I started lingering late at the pub and just started drinking... A LOT.

I was drinking excessively, and it wasn't pretty because it made me even angrier. As a result, I began to lash out at my friends. Not because they were wrong, but because I was so hurt that all I could do was yell at people.

I had a strong relationship between my loneliness and stress. I was lacking social support, and my increasing depression was pulling me back from socializing with people. Money was still an issue, and now my drinking habits were like a cherry on top. I felt so alone in a city of millions, once again.

I had no clue what was going on around me. I was trying my best to stay strong, but I had no strength left to fight my emotions. I could not speak to my family because they were already going through so much, and even if I shared it with Niall, he was not going to solve my problems. I wanted to let it all out, but I had no freaking idea how to.

I knew that simply talking to people about how I was feeling could be an enormous help, but it still couldn't solve my issues. Niall couldn't fix everything, but he was a good listener. And I also didn't want to bother him, so I let it be. But I also needed someone who would listen to me without getting distracted and without judging me. Finally, after about a month, while carrying my emotional baggage, Niall sat me down. That was one thing I cherished about our friendship. He always knew when something was wrong, even if I wouldn't tell him. He saw me drinking heavily and knew I needed help.

After work one night, I was drinking as usual and as heavily. He looked at me and said, "You need to quit your nonsense!"

I got offended listening to him saying that to me. I thought, how dare he tell me how to feel and what to do when my brother had just died. My emotions were at an all-time high level at this point in my life, so when people tried to comfort me and tell me everything is going to be ok, they put me into a rage. He knew I wasn't listening, but he kept telling me this because he knew that eventually, I would.

I knew deep down that my brother was in a better place. His journey was only for him to make it to thirty and then become an angel. He couldn't handle how life was treating him on earth. I know a lot of people who go through the same thing my brother was going through. Mental health is a big thing, and when the ego and the negativity take over, sometimes, you just can't get away from it. During times like these, it is comparatively so much easier to be negative than to be positive. Again, I knew all of this in my head, but my heart wasn't on the same page, and I couldn't help it. It felt like a coping mechanism for me to keep drinking and suppressing my pain.

CHAPTER 4
THE LIGHT IN ME

There was no right or wrong method for me to process the emotions I had been going through. The agony I had been experiencing was unbearable. I was lacking in motivation, which was combined with a reduced emotional response. I was in a condition of profound apathy, but I didn't know how to react to the excruciating pain I was experiencing on the inside.

My life was depressing, to say the least. 'Life happens for you, not to you,' I found difficult to believe. I was discouraged and frustrated. I didn't have the strength to make any decisions to improve my situation. I tried to listen to what Niall said to me, but it was complicated and almost next to impossible to listen to him and act according to it.

Sometimes I blame my life for not giving me the best things. That's why I felt like giving up was an easier option, and I was thinking the same thing at this point in life. I wanted to give up on everything because I had tried so hard to save my brother for so long. When I finally realized that he would not change himself or consider anyone's efforts for him, I gave up on him. And I felt like I just wanted to give up again. I couldn't stop thinking about what had happened to me. I didn't have the same enthusiasm for things that used to excite me.

I imagined that moving to New York City would allow me to do great things and that everyone would appreciate me as a result. Then I found myself in a state of depression living here. I felt like every time I tried to get up, I was immediately knocked down. Then I thought to myself, I wonder if that is how my brother felt. It was all taking a toll on me.

I knew I had to focus and recall my purpose for moving to New York City in the first place. As soon as I realized what I was doing to my life, I knew I had to stop doing that and get myself together. I promised myself that I would work on it again. This time, I was determined not to waste this opportunity and to demonstrate to everyone that my decision was the best one I had ever made. I knew I had to do something for myself to lessen the burden of how I was feeling.

My roommates could see that I was having a tough time going through things. Josh mentioned maybe I should start working out at the gym next to our apartment. I had never been a gym girl, but I was tempted to join because it was so close and would cost only nineteen dollars a month. So, I figured I would give it a go.

I walked into the gym the next day and signed up. It was a small dark ratty-looking place where a bunch of men were lifting weights, like something you would see in a movie. It felt like they were all training for some sort of big fight. I was very put off by the place, and it made me feel awkward. I had no clue what to do at the gym, so I just walked over to the treadmill and started walking. They all just stared at me. By their looks, I could tell that they all were wondering, "what is a girl doing here?" It was terrifying and uncomfortable for me, and I left after forty-five minutes. When I got home, I said to Josh, "never doing that again."

That day, I went on Groupon to see if they had any workout class offers. There were a lot of yoga courses, which surprised me. I tried yoga in Pittsburgh once and didn't know much about it. However, it was thirty-nine dollars for one month of unlimited yoga, and the studio was right by the doctor's office, so I could go after work. I didn't have enough on my plate, working two jobs seven days a week and trying to fit yoga in, but I signed up because I knew I had to do something, and I couldn't return to the same gym again. So, giving yoga a shot seemed like a good option.

My first lesson was on a Saturday, and it was Bikram Yoga, which I had never done before. When I entered the room, it was completely packed. It was above one hundred degrees, and my mat was about a half-inch away from the other person. I didn't mind the heat, but it bothered me that I was so close to someone who was sweating. The class was twenty-six postures spread out over ninety minutes. I was irritated the entire time in class and did not enjoy myself. I became upset because I couldn't even do the postures, and the person next to me was sweating all over my mat. The little drops of someone else's sweat on my mat were driving me crazy.

I felt like I was going to throw up at one point. By the end of the class, I was already a complete mess. I was sweating and feeling queasy when class ended. I went away thinking, "I'll never do that again!"

That day, I went home and didn't feel any better, but I decided to research the yoga I was doing to better understand it. Most articles stated that the first time is difficult and that you must keep practicing, to which I rolled my eyes, but I had already bought the package, so I had to finish the month.

I returned to the class as I had already decided to continue for the rest of the month. I was beginning to feel better, and my body was toning well. I started to notice when I was on the mat, my anxieties vanished, and I was just focused on the current moment. I still didn't enjoy the style of yoga I was practicing, but my mind was becoming less foggy. It was strange, but I thought it was working out fine for me. After attending the class only a few times, I realized my attitude changed from hating to liking it.

When it comes to Groupon or bundles, they are only valid for first-time students. After that, you must pay the full fee, which was too pricey for me. I was so irritated because there was something that made me feel better for the first time in my life, but I couldn't enjoy it because I was broke. I hated the feeling that I couldn't live my life the way I wanted because of money. I wasn't even asking for a lot or any kind of lavish lifestyle that resembles the ones rich people usually have. I just wanted to have a yoga class to keep myself and my mind in the right place.

I was desperate to continue doing yoga, so I found another way of carrying on with it. I signed up for new yoga studios all over the city as a first-time student each month. That way, I didn't have to pay the membership fee, and I could carry on doing yoga without disturbing my financial budget. I discovered another Bikram studio near the pub in Union Square. When I arrived for class, the teacher was wearing a speedo with his hair pulled back. I thought to myself, "what the hell did I get myself into."

When the class began, the teacher was yelling at us through a headset, telling us we were doing it all wrong and needed to work harder. It was as though I was at boot camp. I was dissatisfied with this studio, but at this time, I realized that yoga was a practice and you had to keep practicing. Every time I showed up at class, I would pray that the teacher in the speedo wasn't teaching. Those thirty days flew by much too quickly. I went back to looking for a new studio and discovered one in the same neighborhood, but it was a hot vinyasa studio.

I discovered that vinyasa was more my thing since it was a heated flow into various positions. That I thoroughly loved. I was feeling a lot better at this stage since yoga calmed me down and was a terrific workout. It made me understand how important it was for me to live in the present moment. I can't live in the past, anticipate the future, or always attempt to serve others while ignoring my own needs.

I was mistreating myself, and it was taking a toll on me, but I didn't realize it. I had no idea how terribly I was causing myself damage. However, I don't believe anyone does. I felt so good after my yoga classes since they helped me understand myself better.

I began researching the advantages of yoga and realized that most women store their emotions in the pelvic area, so if you don't exercise that area, you will feel trapped. You'll overthink everything that will keep your emotions out of your control. It is undoubtedly challenging to have too many emotions that are too out of your control. Learning this made me wonder why I wanted to be sad and couldn't handle my emotions appropriately. I'm not claiming yoga will rescue the day and solve all the problems of life, but it is an excellent tool for improving the state of a person's mind and body.

I had been exhausting myself a lot during that time with my jobs and yoga classes, but I didn't mind since yoga helped me in keeping myself on track. I was even developing muscles and doing great physically. I had no idea yoga was a thing because, like many people, including myself, I would have this misconception that people who practice yoga sit about and sing songs. I'm sure there are yoga courses like that, and I applaud those who teach them. Yoga was a great workout for me, and it was quickly becoming my love. I never had a "passion" in my life. I had constantly been working since I was fourteen years old. I had never been in any sport at school or had a hobby. I used to dance at a young age but never had a passion for it. I would not be lying if I said yoga was something I loved and enjoyed. It surely felt nice having something I enjoyed. I was joyful again, but I was worried since I was always expecting the other shoe to drop. I felt like every time something good happened to me, something bad was going to happen immediately after. I knew I needed to get out of that mindset. In yoga, I was reminded daily that I couldn't think the way I was constantly thinking, and I had to keep practicing staying in a positive mindset.

That weekend, I had a Sunday off. I joined my friend Gemma for brunch. I met Gemma through a Pittsburgh connection. She lived in Astoria, so it was nice to have another girlfriend there. It gets a bit tiring living with guys, and your best friend is a guy.

Gemma was the kindest person I had ever met. She would comfort me in every way possible and help me with everything that I needed. She was the kind of person you could always count on. She had all the nice and positive traits that made our friendship even more fantastic. One day, she told me that her roommate was moving out and that I could move in if I wanted. I was still living with the boys at the time, but Astoria was closer to the city, so I said yes without hesitation. I told the boys that weekend that I'd be moving out and would be living with my friend. And just like that, I was a resident of Astoria, Queens.

My new apartment was an older walk-up building. We were on the first floor. The place had plenty of room for us both. Everyone in the neighborhood was friendly and seemed very protective of each other, which I liked. Now that my membership had expired at the studio in Union Square, I needed to find a new location to practice yoga, and I was running out of options in the city.

The weekend I moved in with Gemma, I was roaming around my new neighborhood to get a feel of the area.

There was everything I needed, shops, the subway, restaurants, and yes, a yoga studio! It felt like a sign when I moved in with my best girlfriend and discovered that we lived next to a yoga studio. I joined the studio and made sure I worked a couple of extra shifts at the bar to keep my membership active after the thirty-day period ended.

My personal strength had grown. I was more focused on what I was doing. I felt less anxious and had less muscle tension in my body. When I first began practicing yoga, it helped me gain control of my mind exceptionally well. I was able to control stress and anxiety while remaining relaxed. It also assisted me in improving my flexibility, muscular strength, and overall body tone. One of the biggest advantages of doing yoga was that I learned how to breathe. I know for myself when emotions arise, I forget to breathe or breathe incorrectly, which can cause more damage. It taught me how to stay calm and focus on breathing.

Yoga may seem to be nothing more than stretching, yet it significantly impacted how I felt, looked, and moved. It is more than just bending and twisting your body while breathing. It was a technique that allowed me to enter a state where I could see and experience reality as it was. The sensory body grows as one allows their energies to become exuberant and euphoric. The unity that yoga generates allows people to feel the entire universe as a part of themselves, making everything one.

Yoga enhanced my memory and concentration. It also helped to manage weight, improve flexibility and posture, helped to bring peace of mind, promote self-control, boost immunity, and improve physical attractiveness while increasing self-confidence and self-esteem. It provided me with the skills to make the necessary changes in myself so that I could realize my full potential in life.

I used to believe that concentrating was the most challenging task on the planet. I used to be prone to a vicious cycle of over-worrying myself, which was stressful. Stepping onto the mat allowed me to disconnect from my thoughts, let go of my problems, and reconnect with my body and mind.

Yoga classes also benefitted me with my social skills and helped me engage with other people in the class. Social bonds impacted both my mental and physical health positively. There was one teacher at the studio that I adored. He was a great teacher but also made the class fun for everyone to enjoy. That is exactly what I needed! Yes, I knew I needed to understand the advantages of yoga, but it was nice to be a bit silly about it as well. He always played hip-hop music during class, which made it such a vibe that I enjoyed. It also made me want to attend class constantly.

For me, yoga was the best practice for acknowledging self-love, inner peace, and self-care, which helped me overcome different traumatic phases of my life. The lessons were fantastic, and I adored the teachers. At this point, my mental space was crystal clean. I had very few negative thoughts and was grateful for what I had. I appreciated life and everything that I had. At that moment, I realized this was the adventure I intended to take. This is my life, and the awful things that happened to me are now behind me.

Of course, we all go through difficult times in life and will continue to do so in the future, but I was a more upbeat person who didn't feel depressed or experience as many unpleasant feelings. I also found myself not drinking as much as I was, which was great. I had no desire for it. Obviously, if there was an event, birthday, or brunch, I would drink, but I wasn't staying late at the pub anymore and feeling sorry for myself. I felt once again I was back on track. Sure, I still had a lot of issues in my life. But with yoga by my side, I felt a bit stronger in fighting my ego and the negative thoughts. Those thoughts took over my life for a good amount of time, but with practicing yoga, I felt a glow within myself. I walked around with my head held high, and I felt the sunshine upon me every morning, even if it wasn't out. I was back on my feet and enjoying my present life moments.

CHAPTER 5
BIG LOVE

You know you are happy when you are ready to face challenging situations, accept them, and find joy. I had started enjoying my life again. Gemma and I were living in Astoria and living our lives to the fullest. I decided to do something different for a change, so I signed up for a dating app. I started going on dates, but it never turned into anything more than a few drinks. It was my first time dating in New York City, and it wasn't fun by any means. It was hard to find a guy that wanted a nice relationship, and I knew I wanted one, but I couldn't take the lies they would tell or their ghosting. I never understood why anyone would ghost someone. Why can't they just say they aren't interested and move on?

I met a guy on the app, and we decided to meet, he seemed nice enough in the beginning. However, before our date, he messaged me asking what I was going to wear on the date. I obviously thought it was weird that he was asking me that question so casually when we hadn't even been on our first date yet. So, I responded with jeans and a nice top.

He replied, "I need you to wear a dress for me ad be sexy."

I was shocked by his response. It felt super weird, and I was uncomfortable, so I canceled the date. It was so odd to me how some men acted that way. Yes, I did come across some very nice guys, but I just let it run its course. I was having the time of my life. My new apartment was great, and Gemma and I were having a blast together and put the relationship status on the back burner. But then my life took an interesting turn.

My phone rang as I was leaving yoga class one evening, and it was an unknown number. When I responded, it was an old banker with whom I had worked at the bank when I first arrived in New York City. It had been two years at this point, which was crazy. He told me that the company had merged with another company, and they were searching for an assistant. He asked me if I wanted to join the team. The salary package was fantastic, and I wouldn't have to work two jobs if I accepted the offer. He told me to think about it and call him in a day or two to tell him what I had decided.

I got off the call and said to myself, "I have to do it." So, I accepted the offer the next morning when I called him.

It was unbelievable since I had been fired from this company two years ago, and now they were calling me back. I was so shocked. That week, I met with the doctor to inform her that I would be leaving. It was bittersweet since they were more like my family at the time, and I was devoted to them. When I contacted Connor to inform them, I felt the same way again. They were all thrilled for me, which was good. They threw me a fantastic goodbye party that weekend. Niall was obviously ecstatic for me, but he realized it wouldn't be the same at work. Would our friendship last? It felt like it was the end of an era for me, the pub, and Niall.

I started that next Monday. The location of the firm had changed since they merged companies. It was a very easy commute from my apartment. I was very excited to start this new position and once again felt like my life was back on track. There were a few faces I recognized which was nice, but some of the faces were new as well. I ended up meeting this new guy there; His name was Jack. He was a member of the team with whom I would be working with. He was extroverted, loud, determined, annoying, nice, hilarious, and a hard worker.

His presence energized me. Something about him made me want to be around him all the time. He was such a badass to me. Our team was a nice group of people, and we all worked exceptionally well together. I was becoming quite close with everyone, just as I had become with the doctor and with everyone at the pub. We worked long hours, and I realized that when a person is with people for ten hours a day, five days a week, it is easier for them to tend to form real bonds.

You could say that Jack was the group's black sheep who didn't like to take direction well from someone else, but it somehow always worked out for him. He never wanted to hear anyone's excuse, especially mine.

Anytime I had a question, he would look at me and say, "Just get it done, Amanda," and he meant it.

He never expressed sympathy for anything I did or said, and he didn't want to hear it, which made me try even harder. I would try harder because, for some reason, I wanted to prove to him I could do anything I put my mind to and didn't need his answers to my many constant questions. I had no financial background and had to teach myself a lot, but Jack never cared for my sob story. He told me I needed to take my series seven exam and series sixty-three exam to get a boost in my career. I had no clue what he was talking about, and he was not a guy who wanted to explain it to me, so google worked for me well.

He would come into the office every morning and get me a cup of coffee. Then, we would sit and talk about the day ahead. It was like a morning ritual for us. He was also quite protective of me because I was one of the only females in the company, so he was constantly on my side. He never allowed anyone to treat me badly, which I adored about him. I applied to take the exams and studied relentlessly for months. I had to cut back on yoga because I had to use every waking moment to study. All of this was so brand new to me, and it was a lot of information to learn.

The day had finally come when I had to take the test. I was so nervous about it. I had always been an overthinker, so sitting through a six-hour exam fueled my anxiety. I finally finished, and the next thing I saw was the word 'Fail.'

I was so disappointed with myself and knew Jack was not going to be happy about it either. So, I just sat there for a bit with tears in my eyes because I felt like I really tried hard at this, and obviously, it wasn't hard enough.

I knew I had to call Jack, I forced myself to call him, and he answered with, "Tell me it's a pass."

With trembling lips, I said, "failed."

He was fine with it and suggested that I try again. Whether it was good or bad, we were always there for each other. Now, I had to wait three months to get myself scheduled for the exam. I hired a tutor to help me and signed up for the classes two days a week. I was determined to pass the next time.

For the next few weeks, I spent a lot of time outside the office with Jack. We'd go to happy hours with our co-workers and client dinners and be around each other all the time. I began to develop feelings for this man as someone I truly cared about. The days got longer, and the months became shorter. He began to have a special place in my heart as a close friend. Every morning when we sat with our coffees, he would look at me in such a way that I could never describe in words. I felt safe with him, comfortable, and knew I could trust him. These daily conversations were mainly about work, but after a while, we started talking about our personal lives as well.

He was going through a lot in his life, and he told me how unhappy he was. I was never the person to want or see someone unhappy for whom I really cared about, so I tried my best to be there for him if he needed someone to talk to, which wasn't his strong suit. If it was brought up, it was a very quick conversation, and then he would change the subject. He was becoming my best friend, and I wanted to be there for him. I wanted to make him feel better. I wanted to help him. I knew his heart was breaking every day because he didn't know how to handle what was going on in his life, and I could see it in his eyes daily. I wanted so badly to help this man smile again.

We headed out for a happy hour one Thursday night, it was a hard week for us as I screwed up on a deal earlier in the week, and it was a very stressful time. We stopped at the restaurant in the entryway of our building. This was our 'Cheers' neighborhood bar. We adored the bartender Patricia and made many friends there as well.

It was a typical night, nothing out of the ordinary for us, then out of nowhere Jack looked at me with the most serious look in his eyes and said, "I love you, and I really need you in my life."

He said it where Patricia overheard him. She looked at me, and I looked at her. We both then looked at Jack, mainly because we had no idea where this was coming from.

While any girl would be overjoyed to hear that, I was speechless for a moment. I didn't really know what to say. Then, my mind started pondering, and questions kept flooding my brain.

"Did I love him in that way? Did I love him as a friend?

Was it love, or was it just care?" I asked myself.

We were then interrupted by a few friends who came in, and we carried on with the night. I went home that evening and just kept thinking about what he said. I knew I had feelings for him but wasn't sure what they were yet.

There was a lot for me to process. I was still young, and he had children to worry about. This was a situation I had never been involved in, so I wasn't sure how to handle that. My heart was saying yes, but my head was saying no. And as an over-thinker, I put so many scenarios in my head that it drove me mad.

I went to the office the next morning and told him it would never work since there were too many external issues that would overshadow our relationship if we got into one at the right time. Above all, I told him that I didn't want to upset his children.

"I'm not going to give up on you or us," he said as he stared at me.

We continued as friends with a strong affection for one another. We continued to go out together, there was this energetic pull he had over me. I constantly wanted to be around him. The way he made me feel was such an exhilarating feeling. We both could be ourselves and just have genuine fun together. Our conversations would stem from the deepest thing one can talk about to the silliest thing one could talk about. We couldn't get away from each other, knowing we might have to in the future.

We filled the room with our positive energy and love whenever we were together in one place. The love that was building between the two of us was quite noticeable to all the eyes around us.

Everyone would look at us and say, "We want that. We want to be loved, admired, and respected like that."

Even though everyone was rooting for us, I was still worried as I was just thirty years old and unsure of what I wanted. The external issues were a lot, and I wasn't sure I could handle them. I didn't want to upset his children, but I also couldn't control my emotions, and neither could he. I wanted to make the right decision for everyone involved.

A blackout snowfall struck one night in the thick of winter, trapping Jack and me in the city. We headed out for dinner. The wine was flowing freely, and the discussion we were having was never-ending. The laughing, the banter it was all so genuine, and I loved and relished every minute of it. That night, he looked at me, grabbed my face, and kissed me. He stated that he would not give up on me or us. He told me he would not stop trying until I was completely his.

Later that evening, we went to Patricia's and told her what had happened. She was so happy for us. Everyone was team Jack and Amanda. We continued with her and had the best time; then Jack started screaming in the middle of the bar, "I love Amanda McAdams."

I thought to myself, here we go again, but it was for the whole bar to hear this time. Secretly overcome with joy when he did this, I also thought this man really does love me, and I love him. The smile on his face was from ear to ear, and the light in his eye warmed my heart.

We continued our friendship for a long period, but it was never serious because I couldn't let down that wall. The issue was still there, and it was quite vivid. I knew it wouldn't end well for me. But I knew the love we had for one another was strong.

Despite this, I never agreed to be with him because I didn't think I could manage everything correctly. I was always there for him, just as he was for me, and I wanted to bring a smile to his face every day. I'd do anything to help him and make him feel loved. I was aware what he was going through was wearing him down. Even though I didn't want to, I knew I had to end this. I had always given our friendship my everything and made him happy. I had no reservation. These were feelings of love and care for him. My heart desired to be with him every day, all day, and share a life with him, but once again, my head said no.

When I told him, what I thought would be best for us, he looked at me with tears in his eyes and said, "I will never give up on you or us," as he grabbed my hand. He always said that to me, which, in some weird way, made me feel like we were going to continue to go on like this.

Jack and I continued to go out a lot as usual, and we continued to have our morning coffee and speak about everything that was going on in our lives. Not only did I love this man, but he was my best friend. We also became this force at work. Everyone loved us and loved being around us.

The time finally came for me to retake my series seven and sixty-three exams. I worked so hard on my studies, and with my tutor's help, I was determined to pass this time. I was determined to make Jack proud and progress in my job. My anxiousness was through the roof since it was exam day again.

It was the end of the exam, and the small hourglass was rotating as I pushed submit. When I peeked up after closing my eyes, it said PASS!! I finally finished it, and all my hard work paid off! I couldn't wait to tell Jack.!

He was so pleased with me that he decided we should go out and celebrate.

I was still not sure what it was about this man that made my heart get pulled towards him. It made me question why I was feeling this way. It could be the reason that he loved me profoundly, cared for me, and wanted the best for me. I took him to meet Niall that night. Niall eventually left our pub and began working at another. Niall sprang out of the bar and gave me the tightest hug when we walked in. Jack and Niall immediately got along.

Since Niall was my dearest closest friend other than Gemma, this was important for me that both he and Jack would get along well. So, seeing them together and getting along well was quite heartwarming for me.

After passing the exams, I had to start my new job as an associate. I wouldn't be lying if I said that the quantity of the work, I had to accomplish was very new to me. I was working crazy hours and had to go out for client dinners. I was becoming exhausted and didn't have time for yoga, which calmed me mentally. Our group wasn't producing a lot of money, and I was worried that I'd be laid off by the same company again, so I started looking for other job opportunities.

Jack pulled me into his office one day, and to my amazement, he informed me that the company wanted to let me go once again. We hugged while drinking our crappy New York City coffee and gazed at each other with tears. It was heartbreaking to realize that we would never be a part of one other's lives again. He was my guy the one I loved, trusted, and felt comfortable sharing my life with, and I was the same for him. I thought maybe I should tell him that I could do this; maybe I should tell him that we could be together and work together on the issues. I didn't want to lose him, and my heart was fighting with my head.

My heart was broken, but I knew I had to leave. I will never forget the way he looked at me on my last day. It was a look of sorrow and loss, a look of confusion, a look of love and care. It had been four years of friendship, years of morning coffees, getting deals done, and conversations. The emotions were at their peak, and the tears were rolling down our faces. That was the last time I had seen or heard from Jack.

The loss of what we had did take a toll on me. I felt like there was a hole in my heart. As you know, I have dealt with loss before, but this was different. I had to decide to leave him. He wasn't taken from me like my brother was taken away. I had control over this loss which I felt like it made things much worse.

"Was I going to regret the decision? Was he going to regret it? Will we ever be able to move forward?" I asked myself.

There were so many thoughts that went through my head. I missed that man every day as I went on with my life. My morning coffee was never the same, my happy hours seemed a bit dull without him, and my life just seemed boring. I couldn't help but constantly wonder if he was okay. I knew from yoga that I had to look at this as a positive experience and think of all the good times we had together. I made sure I went to yoga a bit more those next few weeks as I didn't want to get into a bad place again.

CHAPTER 6
RED FLAGS

I had started a new job that I loved. Things were going well, and I hadn't spoken to Jack in a long time. It was both disappointing and understandable. I was still feeling lost without Jack. I just felt like I lost my best friend more than anything. My girlfriends, however, kept getting on me about at least setting up a profile on a dating app, once again. I had experienced dating apps before and just felt like it was a waste of time, but I knew my girlfriends were right when they suggested I make a profile and not take it seriously. More like creating a dating profile just for fun. One day, I was swiping left and right, bored, and matched with a guy named Michael.

We began chatting through messages on the app. He seemed nice and made me laugh, which was something I was always attracted to. He invited me out on a date for dinner and drinks, which I thought was a nice gesture.

My first date with him was quite nerve-racking. My thoughts flashed through many scenarios of how my date might turn out moments before I was set to see him. I started becoming nervous about the date and had no clue why. It could be because I had to hang out with a stranger and have an awkward conversation, or maybe I was somehow attracted to him.

Michael and I were to be meet at a restaurant in Columbus Circle. He was running late, which was great because I was planning to have a drink and wait until my nerves calmed down. He was well dressed and courteous when he arrived. We had a fantastic time enjoying dinner and beautiful evening together. He drove me home, and that was the end of it. I wasn't really in the mood to go out as I was moving into a new apartment in Long Island City the next weekend. Long Island City was the neighborhood next to where Gemma and I lived in Astoria. I would walk there on the weekends because it was by the water and just such a lovely area. I used to walk by the luxury buildings and would tell myself I was going to live there one day. Well, that dream came true. I was finally in a great position regarding work and money. I could move into a luxury apartment on my own. It even had a rooftop pool which I adored. It was a small studio apartment, but I didn't mind as it was just me who was going to live there.

I took my time moving into my new place and loved every minute of making it my own. I had never lived on my own since I moved to New York City, so it was a big deal for me. Michael and I were still in contact, and he even helped me move some of my stuff to the new place. He was pleasant, polite, and attentive. That was something I really liked about him. Being a Leo, I enjoy being the center of attention, especially in relationships, and he always made me feel that way. He would constantly text and call me and always made me feel wanted. About two months into our relationship, he was frequently staying with me. I would ask to stay at his, but he would always have an excuse, mainly because it was too far out in Connecticut. Eventually, his excuses started to seem a bit odd, and all of them started to feel like red flags to me. My gut instinct at that point was starting to tell me something was wrong, but I ignored it.

My heart kept convincing me that he was a terrific person, and it didn't matter at all if he was not inviting me over to his place. That weekend, my friend Patricia and another good friend Mo, whom I met at the restaurant where Patricia worked, asked me to Jersey for the weekend.

I invited Michael to come along and go with me as it had been a few months and I felt like I liked this person, so I wanted to see if my friends would like him as well. I was respectful of Patricia and Mo's opinions as they were my good friends. We had a really good time that weekend, and my friends also enjoyed Michael's company. I really thought to myself maybe I had found a good guy, and things would start to work out well for me in the relationship department.

All was going well with Michael and me, and I was enjoying every bit of our relationship. One night he told me he was heading out for a guy's night, to which I didn't think anything was wrong about it. However, I noticed he had left his iWatch on the counter after he left.

As I stood there staring at it on the counter, I felt the urge to have a look at it. I knew I shouldn't open it or check anything. I knew that wasn't the right thing to do, but my curiosity got the best of me, and I opened it up anyways. It was earth shattering for me to find text messages from another woman. There were messages about coming over and hooking up, which were quite explicit. I felt like someone punched me in the stomach. We were obviously not in love by any means, but I did trust him and thought things were going great, especially after I introduced him to my friends. He returned to my apartment that night, and I immediately questioned him. He didn't seem mad that I went through his watch and explained that it was all a joke which was the dumbest answer I had ever heard.

I feel like when people get caught, they lie and say "oh, we were just joking." These messages weren't a joke, but Michael and his charming ways talked me out of it. However, I told him to leave as I needed some space. I called Patricia and Mo to tell them about what happened that night. Patricia had always been the one to never judged me or anyone.

"Take some time and think about it with a clear mind," said Patricia.

Mo, on the other hand, was a no-nonsense woman, and she told me to dump his ass right then and there. I know we were only dating for a few months, but he made me feel like I was his girl, that I was special to him, and now all of this just seemed so painful.

I didn't talk to him for almost a week. However, my feelings for him made me look like a complete idiot when I texted him one night while I was out drinking with Gemma. She had met Michael a few times before, but she always told me there was something about him that wasn't right.

Every time I ignored her and continued meeting him anyway.

Of course, Michael fooled me into thinking he was done with the other woman and would only be with me one hundred percent from that point onwards. I was manipulated by his lies and decided to give him another shot. He started staying at my apartment and was giving me as much time as possible. He would drive me to work before he would go to his workplace. His schedule always seemed a little unusual to me. I hadn't even met any of his co-workers ever. It was also fishy that he always said the right things to me. I was so blinded by his charm that I never thought that it was a red flag. Nobody could say the right things in front of you unless they are rehearsed or have used the same tactics on someone before. Every time I questioned him about anything, he always had a response that made me think it was so stupid of me to question him in the first place. As a result, I started avoiding bringing up such topics to avoid getting into a fight with him.

His employment situation was bugging me, and my mind warned me that something wasn't right... red flag!! If I were to ask my heart, everything seemed fine and normal to me.

It was like I knew he was doing something wrong in my head, but in my heart, I wanted to believe he wasn't. I liked him so much that I desperately wanted to see the good in him as I always did with everyone. Sometimes I would often think to myself my empathetic heart was more of a curse than a blessing for me!

We had been in a serious relationship for approximately six months when I brought him back to Pittsburgh for the holidays. It was nice to take someone home for the holidays and have someone to share it with.

My parents and Michael got along very well, and we stayed with my mom during my stay in Pittsburgh. Michael was very helpful around the house, which my mom adored about him and appreciated. However, we only stayed at my parents' house for a little while as we decided to split the holiday stays between my family and his. We flew out on Christmas Day and drove straight to his sister's house from the airport so we could have Christmas dinner with them. On the way to his sisters that day, he confessed everything to me out of nowhere. He told me that he was unemployed and didn't have a place to live in Connecticut. He went into detail about how he was recently laid off and was living with his parents. I just sat there and looked at him with confusion. I couldn't believe he was just now telling me all of this. It's been six months! I knew my gut feelings were right, and my head was giving me all the right signals whenever it hung the red flag in front of my eyes that I so carelessly kept ignoring. I knew something was wrong from the beginning!

People always say that you won't be wrong if you believe your intuition, which I believe, but I think women ignore it a lot of the time as we don't want to seem crazy for making any accusation. I didn't know what to say or do as we head to his sisters' house for Christmas, but I wasn't even mad at him for some reason. I knew I should be in my head, but in my heart, I felt bad for him. People get laid off all the time. I certainly did in the past, so I didn't want to judge him because of that. I thought if my parents lived in New York City when I got laid off, I would move back in with them too. I didn't want to make the situation worse, but I knew I was going to have a tough time trusting him going forward.

Then things went from bad to worse. I've always been the kind of person that fights to make a relationship work. I think it stemmed from seeing my parents get a divorce at a young age. I wanted to help them and fight for their relationship. So, I set out on a quest to help Michael. I told him not to worry and that he could stay with me if he wanted. I also told him I would help him financially until he got back on his feet.

It would only be fair at this point to think that I was beyond stupid to be offering all kinds of comfort to Michael even though he had been lying to me about so many things all this time.

Things were going alright until, once again, another situation came up. Lately, we had been going out a lot, and it was only me who was paying for all the meals and outings, which had taken its toll. He then started paying a lot for things out of nowhere. He told me that the firm where he used to work owed him money and that he could now pay his bills. I went along with it for a while, but my intuition told me something wasn't quite right, and I knew from last time that I should trust my gut instead of him.

A weekend later, I planned a nice dinner for myself and my friends Phillip and Tony from the pub would be there, meeting Michael for the first time. It was a lovely meal, and we all decided to split the cost of it. I noticed Michael got up and walked over to the waitress just as the bill was about to arrive. I didn't give it a second thought. After a few minutes, something strange happened.

"Are you Barbara?" The waitress approached me and whispered in my ear.

"What do you mean?" I questioned her in confusion.

She explained that Michael had given her a credit card under the name Barbara.

"No, I'm not," I told her.

However, I knew who Barbara was... It was his mother. So, after four vodkas, I shouted at him at the table, which everyone overheard, and Tony, the gentleman that he is, ended up paying for the meal. I was completely humiliated. Michael and I had been dating for nearly a year, and I was at a loss for words. I told him to stay with his mother as I didn't want him at my apartment. I knew I had been such a fool to still stay with him in the relationship, but I cared for him so much for some reason. I knew what he was trying to do was wrong, but once again, he talked me out. He brought on the sob story and the charm that he just wanted to do something nice for my friends and me. He told me he felt bad that I was the one to be always paying for the meals whenever they went out. He told me he would pay his mom back all the money once he gets the job. He kept selling his stories to me, and I kept buying every bit of what he said.

He was like a drug to me, and I simply couldn't get rid of him, even if I wanted. Our relationship had so many red flags, and I fed off the chaos. The following week I received a call from AMEX that there were a few charges on my card they didn't recognize. Furious, as I knew it was Michael, but how did he have my AMEX? I confronted him about it and said he must have used it accidentally. I had sent him the number once to book something for me, and I am assuming he saved the number. He kept apologizing about it, and I was completely lost at this point. Who does this type of stuff?

After all the mayhem, he invited me to dinner one night, which I accepted. He kept going on and on about how sorry he was and that he will pay me back. He successfully sold another story to me when he said that the lack of employment took a mental toll on him. Obviously, I fell for it again! He knew I would give him another shot if he gave me a sob story. I just sat there and rolled my eyes at his bullshit. At this point, this guy had become a successful manipulator, a narcissist, and someone who could not be trusted. He walked over to the waitress to pay after dinner. I already knew he didn't have any money. So, I shouted at him, telling him he couldn't use his mother's credit card again. He assured me he wouldn't.

For a long period, we went through this cycle and the got much worse. But I couldn't stand it any longer and told him we needed to take a break. I spent my time doing a lot of yoga while he returned to his mother's. That week, I met Niall for drinks and told him what was going on. He had met Michael before and didn't like him at all. He constantly claimed that there was something wrong with him. I told him everything, and he was furious that I had stayed.

The 'you are better than this' lecture was delivered to me. Niall had my back even though he knew I wouldn't listen to him.

"Let him cause another problem, and I'll take care of this," said Niall.

As I was heading to yoga one day, I received a notification on my phone from a girl named Lisa to accept her request on Find Friends App. It seemed strange to me. Michael was the only person I utilized this app with since he always lied to me about where he was, forcing me to phone the bars hunting for him. I wasn't sure what to make of that, but I checked because her last name was also included and sounded very familiar.

I walked out of class and called my phone company to see if they could help me figure out how to deal with it.

They said that whoever owns that Apple account on their phone added you as a friend. I sat there for a long time, attempting to decipher the situation like it was The Da Vinci Code. Then I realized, "Holy shit!!!" Lisa was the same girl Michael was receiving messages from when I checked his iWatch about a year ago!

He must have been with her and obtained her Apple information, including her AMEX number. I didn't have proof, but I decided to go with my gut feeling as it had been working correctly for a long time.

I found her on Facebook and sent her a message. I have always been the type of person to get answers immediately, and I knew he would lie to me straight away, so I took matters into my own hands. I introduced myself and informed her that I was with Michael and that he had her AMEX card. She immediately messaged me talking about him. I wasn't much surprised that she did not have anything good to say about him.

She said that she went through her AMEX statement and saw a slew of transactions she didn't recognize. One of them was the dinner we just had when I asked him not to use his mom's card, and he said he didn't. Well, that was because he used Lisa's apple pay! She told me about all his misdeeds and how he was cheating on another woman and me, besides herself. I wasn't sure if I was shocked by this news or not. Michael knew exactly what he was doing, and he was a true manipulator to these other women as well, just like he was with me.

It was all a whirlwind. Finally, I confronted him with the whole truth! Of course, he denied everything, and I was done with him. That, on the other hand, he would not accept. I had to put him on a no entry list since he would constantly show up at my apartment building. This went on for months, and it was both difficult and terrifying. Many nights, I was scared he would show up and cause a scene. I did my best to ignore him and eventually changed my phone number. Ultimately, he did end up vanishing from the face of the earth.

My mental health, personality, and self-esteem all suffered due to being in such a toxic relationship with Michael. These adjustments have varied from a general sense of unease in his environment to despair and anxiety.

I was becoming more damaged by staying with him but getting rid of him was one of the best decisions I had ever made.

One of my most difficult and emotional moments was my breakup. It had thrown my entire universe into disarray and elicited many painful and disturbing feelings. It was a loss for me, not just in terms of the partnership but also in the shared ambitions and promises. Every love relationship starts on a high note of anticipation and expectations for the future. I'd gone through a lot of disappointment, worry, and heartache. I really thought this could have been something. I thought I could fight and help him. But I could not be more wrong about it.

Recovering after a breakup may be tough and time consuming because of the sorrow, interruption, and uncertainty. However, I knew it was critical to continually tell myself that I could and would overcome this adversity and even go forward with newfound hope and optimism. I was a strong woman and started looking for things that made me genuinely happy. I had always been a very confident person, but for some reason, in my relationship with Michael, I felt so insecure and lost myself. I lost that Amanda who had the glow about her, the one to see the sunshine every morning. All the chaos I was addicted to put me in a very bad place. Oddly enough, when I ended that chaos, I felt even more lost. I wonder what sense that even makes. One would think I would feel better without him, but it was completely the opposite.

The only silver lining was Lisa. Soon after we became friends, she was quite grateful that I reached out to her. After that, I had no desire to date anybody else since I couldn't believe anything anyone said. As a result, I've realized that I need to start recognizing red flags, stop wearing rose colored glasses and surely cease to think the best of people every time. Although it was very sad to me as I wanted to believe all people are good.

CHAPTER 7

NEW YORK CITY ANGEL

After my encounter with Michael, I decided to take a break from dating. I did enjoy being in a relationship, but I just couldn't go through something like that again. The thought of getting back on the dating apps and going out on dates was just something I didn't want to do. I felt like just giving up on it. Work was going well, and life was getting back to normal. I felt as if I was in the present moment and had a more general sense of how I felt about life overall. I was more linked to experiencing positive feelings than negative ones. I was satisfied with all areas of my life, especially at work.

I was living the life that I had always wanted. I had a great job, a luxury apartment, and a good core group of friends. I always knew that things would get better, and I could deal with what was happening. In short, I was able to feel happy again. But life always has some unpredictable challenges, and that is exactly what was about to happen to me, something that I was completely unaware of.

It was a typical Monday at work, and I was busy. That afternoon I received a text from Connor that said, "I'm very sorry, Amanda," I had no idea what he was talking about, so I texted back, but he didn't respond. I went into a conference room and dialed his number right away. When he answered, he seemed distraught and simply kept saying sorry. I started feeling very anxious and kept asking him what had happened.

When he finally broke the ice, he said, "It's Niall... He passed away last night."

At first, I didn't know what he was saying. I kept saying that he had been mistaken and nothing happened to Niall. But then he said that Niall drowned in Long Beach, Long Island, the night before. It took me a long time to understand what he was saying to me. I dropped my phone and fell to the floor, uncontrollably sobbing. I lost my ability to think about anything. I couldn't breathe. I picked up my phone and called the friend that he was with as I was sure that all of that had to be a mistake.

His friend answered and said, "Amanda, I am so sorry," my brain froze listening to him. He continued, "Yes, it is true. Niall has passed away."

I couldn't catch my breath. Niall was dead. I immediately called my mom, screaming into the phone like she did when RJ died. I couldn't get the words out of my mouth. I didn't want to say it. I just kept crying and screaming. My mom and Niall were close, as was I to his family. She was in utter shock, and I just hung up. I contacted Anthony, my co-worker, to grab my belongings from my desk and bring them to me.

As I was crying on the floor, he burst into the conference room and hugged me. My boss followed behind him to come in and console me as well. I couldn't get up from the floor, I was curled up in a ball on the floor of a conference room, hysterical, and I didn't give a shit what my boss or anyone else was saying to me. They kept trying to help me up, but all I wanted to do was just lay there and cry. My heart was shattered, like a piece of me was taken away from me forever.

I had no idea what to do. I was lost and had no clue where I should go. Anthony escorted me outdoors to the park, where we sat for a while. It was nice of him to try to console me, but again everything he was saying was going in one ear and out the other. I knew I needed to call everyone, notably Manny, as we were a trio. Recently though, Manny decided to move back to California, and Niall and I were already very sad about it. We knew we were going to miss him loads.

Dialing his number at that moment, knowing what I was about to tell him, made me want to throw up. He answered in his cute happy voice, and all I could say was, "Niall is dead!"

His response was the same as mine: it had to be a mistake. Manny was just in New York City a few days ago, and we went to visit Niall at the bar he worked at. All we kept saying was, how did this happen, and why did this happen?

I knew my next call had to be Niall's dad Ray. I know I should have called him first, but I just couldn't bring myself to do it. That was the reason I decided to call Manny first. I dialed his number crying hysterically in the middle of Madison Square Park. That was one thing about New York City there were millions of people there, and at that very moment, not one person existed as they passed me there on the bench crying. The grief I heard over the phone from Niall's father was something I'll never forget. By the end of the conversation that we were having on the call, he took a small pause and said, "Amanda, he loved you so much."

We all gathered at a pub owned by one of our friends that night. The regulars and close friends from the pub. We all simply sat there crying and in complete shock. My best friend had died, and I couldn't believe it. I knew I needed to go into business mode once again, especially because Niall's father was in Ireland, his mother was in the South of France, and his sister was in Australia.

That night, I had to make many calls and sort out the logistics. We were then told that we needed to identify the body and collect his belongings. His sister Sharon, with whom I had a strong relationship, arrived first at JFK and requested if I might accompany her for the identification. Her boyfriend, and another friend of Niall's, joined us as well. My emotions the whole way there were overwhelming. Was I really driving to the coroner's office to ID my dead best friend?

That is something I sincerely hope no one should ever experience. It was the saddest thing I ever had to witness. We felt sick to our stomachs as we came out of the corner office. The pain in my heart felt like someone was stabbing me repeatedly, and the tears would not stop. I was in so much pain, and I did my very best to try to hide it as I knew his family was going through so much worse than what I was going through.

I have a mechanism in life where I sometimes try to be funny when I am upset or see people I love upset, so I tried to do that. The sight of his sister sobbing the way she was, brought about a lot of memories of my brother, and to watch her in such pain was utterly heartbreaking for me. I could feel her pain and understood it, but I knew if I had told her that at that exact moment, she would not grasp what I was saying to her.

Niall's death was the most devastating experience that had ever happened to me. I know my brother's death should be, but Niall and I were closer than RJ and I ever were. Losing Niall felt like I had lost a piece of myself. I couldn't even describe the pain to its fullest. We walked away from the coroner's office that day with very heavy hearts.

Sharon looked at me and said, "There aren't many of his belongings left, but I'd like you to have his watch."

Listening to Sharon broke my heart further into millions of pieces. I sobbed my eyes out uncontrollably. At that moment, I thought I could never be the same person again, and my life would never be the same with such an important person missing from my life.

The next several days were difficult. His father and mother had finally arrived in New York City. They wanted the funeral to be held in Ireland, but they also wanted a memorial ceremony in New York City. Niall had a deep affection for New York City as if they were soul mates. He was enamored with the culture, the people, and everything else. He was the poster child for New York City. He loved this city so much, and it loved him right back.

He was a very bright spot in everyone's life, bringing out the best in everyone. I know that our friendship was unlike any other I'd ever experienced. He always made sure I was okay and really was the only person I trusted in New York City other than Jack when we were so close.

He provided me with comfort whenever I needed it, as he was good at listening and empathizing. He always showered me with big hugs and listened to all my problems. He had words of genuine encouragement, compassion, and reassurance. His physical gestures of affection and verbal expressions of sympathy were all I needed during the difficult times of my life. All the things he did for me, and I did for him were beyond comparison, making our friendship nothing short of beautiful. Even as I write this, I can't even get most of the words out that described our friendship and who Niall was as a person.

We also wanted to raise funds to send him back to his family in Ireland. I had no idea how much anything like that would cost. I opened a Go Fund Me account, and his friends and I started raising money for his family. We were also introduced to a foundation that assists families in sending them back to where they're from.

That family started this foundation because they had a child who passed away in a car accident in New York, and they had difficulty transporting them home, so they established a charity to assist others. They cover the costs, and you collect funds for the charity. The Go Fund Me campaign grew in popularity as the week progressed. We ended up raising $32,000 for Niall's family and the foundation, which was very helpful. Finance is the last thing a family wants to deal with when they just lost someone close. I saw my parents go through it when my brother passed away.

It was the day of the memorial, and I arrived early. The knot in my stomach was an overwhelming feeling. To have to be there and try to celebrate Niall's life was going to be very hard. We put together a beautiful memorial, and the number of people who showed up was amazing. We decided that we would do a video of pictures and have a few people speak about Niall. I was also asked to speak, and of course, without any hesitation, I agreed to it. During the memorial, everything was getting to me, watching the photos, and seeing his family in pain. I was losing it. It was my turn to speak, and I couldn't. I said no and just walked out the door. Ray followed behind me, and we sat on the bench outside the pub with tears in our eyes.

He looked at me and said, "You know Amanda, the love he had for you was so deep."

I looked at him and said the exact same thing back. We sat there for a while, and at one point, we even stopped talking. We just sat there in silence. Just sat there like Niall was sitting with us. His family was always so happy that he and I were so close, as well as my family. Everyone around us felt that energy between us.

He was the first person I met in New York City who was full of life and was everything to me for a long time. We had a strong affection for one other, but not in a romantic sense. I never imagined that guys and girls could be that close without sexual feelings. We never felt sexually attracted to each other. Rather we were so close to each other, like true friends. He treated me with lots of respect, and that is something hard to find in New York City.

The funeral was to take place in Ireland, and the worst thing was that I couldn't go as flights were exceedingly expensive only a few days prior. That really wore me down, but I knew he was in heaven, telling me not to spend that money. I also knew that I would spend the rest of my life regretting that decision.

Over the next few weeks, I couldn't get out of bed because I was so devastated. For days, I just sat in my pajamas, wearing his watch. Patricia called and suggested that we should meet in the pub and that I must eat and be in the company of others. Niall was her favorite. There wasn't a single person on the earth who didn't adore him. I went to the pub, took one glance at her, and burst out crying. She looked at me and did the same, and we simply hugged each other.

I kept asking her why. What caused this to happen? Why did my best friend die so young? Niall had just celebrated his thirtieth birthday a few months before his death, and people from all around gathered to celebrate. His entire family was there for him as well. It was as if he realized he was about to leave this world and wanted to have one final get-together with us all. It was a party of a lifetime.

So many of my friends tried to help me in getting through this difficult period in my life, but I couldn't listen. It didn't matter to me what they were all saying to comfort me. They could never fill the void Niall left in my heart with his sudden death. Everyone kept telling me that he's in a better place now. Which, to me, was bullshit. My brother seemed to be in such a poor position here that he was in a better place when he passed away. That was not the case with Niall. I felt that he was taken and that there was no cause for it. Every day, the memories of Niall haunted me.

Days, weeks, and months started to pass, and everyone kept telling me that time will heal everything, which I thought was again bullshit. I felt like it was getting worse over time. I kept looking at pictures, and the pain kept growing. I was kept in a very difficult rut of loss and grief.

How can someone move on from such grief, though? How can someone cease the memories from pouring into every situation they go through daily? I couldn't even walk into an Irish pub and hear an Irish accent without bursting into tears. My soulmate had vanished, and I felt betrayed.

I knew I had to get on with my life, which sounds so terrible. I had to go back to work. I had to stay professional. Only one thing I knew would help me overcome that grief. So, I started doing yoga again, which was helpful. The feeling was still there, like a knot in my throat. I started to write about it and made sure I went to yoga at least twice a week. After a while, I realized that Niall was there in my life for a specific reason. We are born with a journey of our own to cover, we can't change it or predict it. It is our journey, and that is that. I truly believe that Niall's journey was to be put in my life to help me and others.

I was supposed to meet him that day in the pub with his big head of curls and those baby blues. We were supposed to have this great friendship for a short time. It was meant to be. He was a part of my journey, just as I was a part of his. I know that a day will never go by without a thought of him. I know that there will always be a special place in my heart for him, even though his absence had left a void, a hole in my heart.

CHAPTER 8

ROSE COLORED GLASSES

After Niall passed away, I knew I had to keep myself busy. My last relationship with Michael really took a toll on me as well. The loss of Jack, then the loss of Niall, and the mental damage Michael did to me were all very infuriating. I was not in a good place and felt very alone. I did not know why I did this, but I returned to the dating apps. It was like I was seeking more pain to suppress the loss I had witnessed.

Dating in New York City was one of the hardest things I have ever experienced. Everyone was on the dating apps, and they could be whoever they wanted to be and live some sort of double life which is what I experienced while dating Michael. I knew I just had to keep trying, but playing these games was just not something I was looking for.

There are more women than men in New York City, which is why dating was more challenging. Most men are young and are just looking for a random hook-up, then there are the men that are married and looking to live a separate life with a girlfriend. There are even guys like Michael who just create a whole other life and hope you don't figure it out. It is like searching for a needle in a haystack.

It was almost summertime in New York City, which I always enjoyed, so I guess it would be nice to have a night out or a nice brunch with someone. One day, while constantly swiping left, I came across the profile of a guy named James. He was attractive and British. I had always enjoyed an accent. I swiped right, and it showed that we were a match straight away. I wasn't excited, to be honest, not because of him. I just wasn't in the mood.

Within the hour, he sent me a message. He appeared extremely kind, but I thought, don't they all appear to be nice and kind when you meet them online? So, we started messaging, and there was some great banter, which I usually like. He asked me on a date, and I said yes. I mean, what do I have to lose? Just one date, then I could go back home and hide in my little bubble. We scheduled the following Monday night to meet up.

It was the weekend of Pride in New York City. Through my friend Anthony, I have made many friends in the LGBTQ+ community. It is such a loving community, and I cherish the friendships I have. That Saturday was the parade, so we were all out for it. Anthony introduced me to a group of his friends with who I immediately became very close. I told them all about my horror stories of dating, and they told me theirs. Since we all had that one thing in common, we all became close quickly. I did, however, tell Kiki about the new guy James.

Kiki said, "Amanda, you deserve to go have a nice evening with a nice man."

The five of us reminded me of Sex and the City. We were all always together and quite protective of each other. I was a part of a family with these men. I felt safe with them. I felt like I was able to just be myself for once. I didn't have to help or think about anyone else before myself when I had been with these people. I didn't have to worry about what anyone thought of me. I could just be happy, Amanda, and have a genuinely good time. It was a very refreshing feeling.

Monday finally came after a long-dreaded hangover from the pride parade. We were to meet at The Beekman Hotel for cocktails and then dinner at Chinese Tuxedo. I wore a lovely blouse with a long pencil skirt and my tallest heels. I arrived early because I prefer to relax and enjoy a drink. As I sat there for about fifteen minutes, James walked in. I was delighted to see that he was dressed very well, unlike a typical New Yorker.

He had the loveliest British accent, which I adored. We had an amazing evening together, and the conversation was simply wonderful. It was like I had known him for years. He began telling me about how he was brought up in London and about his current job in New York. I found his story quite intriguing. I was glad we still had dinner to go to as I didn't want to leave yet. He had that amazing vibe around him that would captivate anyone's mind, and he could certainly chat to everyone without making them bored. I couldn't deny the fact that he was indeed very charming. However, I was unsure whether it was a red flag. He was very polite, and everything about him and the evening felt lovely.

With everything that seemed so perfectly fine with this man, I couldn't help myself from questioning if all of that was true or if I was just wearing rose-colored glasses again as I did with Michael. I hated comparing what we didn't even have yet to my past relationship.

We continued the great conversation, accompanied by some laughter while enjoying our dinner. I really enjoyed the time together with James. We called it a night at a decent time. By the end of our date, he kissed me on the cheek, and we went our own ways. On my way home, I felt happy. I thought that this date would be a nightmare, but to my surprise, it turned out great! He texted me the following day, saying he needed to see me. I told him I only had time for lunch, so he planned a small picnic outside my office in a nearby park. It was adorable! We had a quick bite, and then off he went back to the Hamptons.

It was a few weeks of us chatting and hanging out. I was really enjoying his company. It was a Wednesday night, and he gave me a call after work. He started the conversation with, "I have something to tell you."

My first reaction was, "Here we go again!!"

He told me he got a DUI about a year ago while driving home from a wine tasting.

He went on to tell me that it was not the only problem. The other problem was that he was placed on probation, and because he moved to a different apartment after it happened, he didn't have any of the information he needed to show them, and now he had to go to court the next day to resolve everything.

It was easier for me to believe what he was saying. Once again, I did not lift my rose-colored glasses and kept them on. I believed him and pretended everything was good. He called me before the court that morning, and that was the last time I heard from him. I spent the entire day without hearing from him. I called him many times and sent him several text messages, but there was no response, which was very unusual as he had never done any such thing before. So many thoughts crossed my mind. I wondered whether all of that was happening between us was all staged to get me to spend time with him or what. The series of doubts were only there for some time, and soon I became concerned since it comes with a package when you are an empathic person. Being a compassionate and empathetic person, I would never want anyone to be in danger. I immediately contacted the police station where he lived to inquire, and they confirmed that he had been arrested, because he didn't follow the probation order that was still in his old mailbox.

I was in shock!!! I called my mom as I felt so terrible for him. He must be so scared! He was alone because his entire family lived in London. I told my mom that I needed to see him in jail. It is even hard to believe that I planned on driving to prison to see a person I went on two dates with.

"I'll come with you," said my mom.

"No, mom," I replied. "You don't have to do this. I'll go alone."

I phoned the jail to gather all the necessary information for my visit. James had no idea what I was doing since I couldn't reach him, and he didn't have my phone number. I traveled out to the jail where he was on Saturday, which was one of the worst of them all. I was terrified and spent the entire time on the phone with my mom. Finally, I parked and entered the jail. It was a terrifying experience for me since I had never visited a jail in my entire life. I was also confused as I did not know what to do. I checked in, put my belongings in a locker, and sat alone with my head down as I didn't want to make eye contact with anyone. The next thing I knew, a woman came up to me and said, "What is your man in for?"

"DUI," I said with a trembling lip.

"Oh, girl, that's nothing. My man is in for homicide."

I wanted to bolt out the door right then and there. When it was time to go in, they placed us in a cage-like room, and we watched the inmates enter the room to their assigned seats. I watched James step out, and he looked so sad. We were let out one by one to sit in our assigned seats across from the inmates, separated by glass. He was shocked I was there. At this point, we were only really talking for about three weeks. He was so happy I came to help him as he had no one. I made sure he was okay, but I knew this was going to be a long road for him.

He told me that he had spoken with his lawyer and that he would be released in two weeks. Hearing him say that made me feel a bit better. Then, he gave me his lawyer's number. I wrote it on my hand with a pen that one of the guards gave me. I knew, in my heart, I needed to help this man.

I opened an account for him so that I could call him and put money on his commissary. Amanda's business model was in full force! I was leaving for Cabo the next weekend with my girlfriends, but I felt better knowing it would only be for two weeks. Every day, we communicated.

"Amanda's BF is calling from jail," the girls would say as we all sort of joked about it, and I joked about it. James called as I was boarding my trip back from Cabo. There was just one week remaining. He started that conversation with there is something I need to tell you. My thought was, "Oh no, not again!"

He went on to explain that after his two weeks, they would be sending him to an ICE detention center as he wasn't a citizen of the United States. He also said he would be facing deportation and would be sent back to the UK.

Now, here is where things get sticky. James was not an American citizen. He had a visa but did not have citizenship in America. Therefore, no matter how little, you risk being deported when you commit a crime. I was both surprised and disappointed. My heart broke for him as he had to go through all the hassle and then now be transferred to ICE. I knew, on that phone call, I had no choice but to fight for him!

I thought that was the worst, but I did not know that something even worse was waiting for me. The next time I went to see him, I discovered that his court date was repeatedly pushed back, and he would now be imprisoned for approximately two months. We were both shocked. All the lawyers kept saying that they were sorry. James had nothing else to do but just wait.

It was very infuriating when you have to let someone sit in jail with your hands tied, and you cannot do anything about it. If that wasn't enough, James told me since he wasn't getting out in two weeks, I would have to get his phone and wallet and contact his family in London.

I didn't understand what James was expecting when he asked me to do this. What was I supposed to tell them? "Hello, this is Amanda. Your son is in prison!!!"

However, I said, okay. I couldn't leave this man alone in prison. Since I had this dire need to prioritize others over myself, I agreed to give his parents a call. So, I went to his house and took his phone and wallet. I opened the phone to get all the contacts I needed, and of course, the jaded girl that I was, I went through his phone. There were a few texts and emails that bothered me. I did come to find out that he wasn't truthful with me about a lot of stuff which was upsetting, but then I thought I only knew this man for a few weeks, so maybe he just didn't feel comfortable telling me a lot of things that early. Again, I put my rose-colored glasses on and moved on with my fight to get him out.

I called his mom and sister to let them know what was happening and that I would do everything to help him. His parents were older and unable to travel. They felt a little better when they knew that someone was in the States fighting for their son and the fact that he wasn't alone. I was also in contact with a childhood friend of his in the UK who was very helpful and supportive, so I was grateful for him.

James and I talked a lot on the phone over the next few weeks. We even wrote letters back and forth to each other. I knew he was lying about his past, which really did bother me as I went deeper through his phone and found out more. I did write him about what I found and that I wasn't okay with it. We had a long talk about it, but all we really could focus on was getting him out. This went on for three months. I drove to jail every weekend to visit him, which was such a weird feeling for me.

Finally, I found him an immigration lawyer and worked tirelessly to have him released from ICE. Because immigration was such a significant deal at the time, the lawyer was able to get his ICE court date moved forward. They would constantly forbid James whenever he said he would pay for himself to return home. The lawyers strictly instructed him to wait until they would say anything.

Watching him go through the process was an incredible eye-opener as to how things are handled in our judicial system. It was utterly heartbreaking.

We eventually received his court date after I battled tooth and nail every day. The offer would be to deport him back to London with the prospect of returning in ten years. I phoned the police officer who was supposed to transport him to JFK as I needed to drop off his luggage with him. He was a very nice man and apologized for going through all of this. At this point, it was a little over three months that he was in jail when they told him it was only going to be two weeks. He went back to London and landed safe and sound.

That weekend, I traveled to London to visit him. At the airport, we hugged and sobbed a little. We immediately went to his parent's place right from the airport. His mother hugged me when I stepped in and began weeping and thanking me.

"Thank you very much for rescuing my son," she said.

I had a great time in London, and we really enjoyed our time together. James would tell me daily about how grateful he was to me for rescuing him from prison. Obviously, I appreciated his kindness.

After that week, I went back to New York City. We continued our long-distance relationship and worked on dating that way, but several warning signs kept popping up. I continued to wear my rose-colored glasses and ignore them as I just wanted so desperately, for once, to be in a relationship where everything would work out fine. This long-distance thing was quite tough on us as a couple. We decided to take a trip to Ireland, which I was very excited about as I was going to surprise Niall's dad!

I always loved Ireland, and knowing Ray was there alone, I tried to make it there as much as possible. We spent a few days in Dublin. My cousins were also there that weekend, so it was nice to spend some time with them as well. We took the train to Limerick that Saturday. When I stepped off the train, I felt the little hairs on the back of my neck stand up. It was like Niall knew I was in his hometown. It really brought up so many emotions. Ray had no idea I was coming since I planned the surprise at his favorite pub. James, my cousins, and I walked into the pub that night.

I walked up behind Ray and asked, "Excuse me, sir, may I buy you a pint?"

There was an utter shock on that man's face! He was in complete disbelief, and tears rolled down his cheeks. He couldn't believe I made the trip for one night to say hi to him. We had a great time, and Ray and I talked for hours about Niall. It was heartwarming and sidetracked me from what was happening with James and me.

James and I got to the airport the next day, and I just couldn't shake all the things I found out. There was a good bit of lying on his part, but like the little white lies turned into bigger ones. I knew, at that moment, I needed to take the rose-colored glasses off and end this relationship. I knew it wasn't going to end well, and I didn't want to be hurt again. We agreed on this, and I hugged him and boarded my plane. That was the last time I saw James.

I was finally back in New York City, and at this point, I was beyond done dating. That weekend, I went out with Kiki, Cici, Gigi, and Anthony. They were aware of James' situation. They, of course, wanted it to work out but knew I did the right thing for my future. They all agreed and told me that maybe I should just be alone for a while and get back to being "Amanda."

They suggested to me that I should do things I want to do and stop focusing on relationships for some time. They told me it would happen when I wasn't looking for it. I agreed with them, but I knew deep down I wasn't really listening and knew I was going to make another bad dating decision.

After James, I went back on the dating app once again. I even tried a matchmaking service. Unfortunately, I was going on terrible dates. I met a few guys I thought I liked, but they went sideways as usual. I was now starting to get a bit of a complex. I constantly asked myself why I was getting myself in these terrible situations with men. Why did I always end up getting hurt? I thought maybe I was just too nice and soft with people, whereas I needed to learn how to be more of a "bitch." Although I knew that it was something I would never be good at. It was as if I was attracted to chaos and drama with these men. I had never been like this when I was living in Pittsburgh. I guess it was New York City making every aspect of life chaotic because it is such a chaotic city. I felt like I needed some serious answers.

CHAPTER 9
BIG HEARTBREAK

I always wanted to be in a relationship, which is the only reason I always stayed in toxic relationships. I love being loved. But going through all the heartbreak really jaded me. I felt like I couldn't trust anyone. As a result, I categorized all men into a cauldron of cheaters and liars. I knew this way of thinking was not good for me or my future, but I just couldn't get past it. I knew I was intelligent and capable of having a healthy relationship, but for some reason, I always gravitated toward chaos. I felt like chaos was normal.

I'd had enough with dating. The past few years and experiences really did a number on me, and I knew I had to return to being the old "Amanda" I was. I needed space and time for myself. I needed to get back into yoga and take care of myself.

It was summer again a year later. I was back doing yoga and having a good time with my friends. I was feeling a little better about where I was in life and where I was heading, regardless of being single.

My phone rang one morning while I was leaving for yoga. I looked down, and to my surprise, I saw his name. It was Jack, believe it or not! I haven't spoken to him in four years. What would I say? It took me a while to respond since it had been so long. But just hearing his voice made me smile. The first thing out of his mouth other than how are you was, "I'm moving into the city."

I was happy for him, not because of the thought that maybe I would see him more, but because he seemed a bit lighter, like some of his stress was gone. He went on to ask me for drinks, and I still felt a bit unsure as it was a sticky situation. I didn't want to get involved in that, so I told him I was busy and couldn't meet him.

A week went by, and Jack kept calling and texting every day to ask me out for drinks, for a walk, for coffee, whatever it would take for me to say yes. I knew that this man would not take no for an answer and would keep on trying until I would say yes. I finally agreed to drinks that Thursday. We met at a bar on the Hudson River that was outdoors. I walked into the bar that evening and saw him sitting there. He looked the exact same. He looked up, saw me, and the biggest smiles came across both our faces.

I sat down, ordered a drink, and we went right into it. I mean, it had been four years since I saw this man. We didn't skip a beat. It was right back to how it was when we had our morning coffee conversations. I also told him about my dating nightmares. He had also been dating all this time, so he shared his experiences with me as well. So many emotions were flooding in. The banter, the conversation, the laughs, everything felt nice. It was like the good old days, which were very comforting for me at that time as I felt so defeated by men in general. It was an easy, fun night, and we both went home. I really did enjoy myself that night. I didn't think much of it, though, as I had been through hell in the past and was enjoying being alone, but he was not like the one to give up that easily, so he kept asking me out. I said no a lot of times, but in the end, he would charm me into saying yes.

That next week I had a blind date planned, and I was not excited about this date at all, but my friend Patricia set it up, so I told her I would go. It was Thursday night, and I was supposed to be meeting this guy on a rooftop. I showed up early as usual to my habit. He walked in, and I immediately sensed that he wasn't my type. We ordered a drink and started chatting. Everything he was saying felt like nails dragged all over a chalkboard. He kept telling me how rich he was. His sense of humor wasn't even appropriate, as I found most of his jokes to be gross! I was not amused with the way he spoke to me or his presence and wanted to get out of there ASAP. When he went to the bathroom, I texted Jack asking if I could come over. He lived close by, so it was convenient for me to sneak out and get to his place. He responded quickly that he was also on a date, but I could go and hang out at his apartment. I asked for the check and quickly started walking toward the elevator. He walked with me and cornered me in the elevator to try and kiss me. I pushed him off me, the elevator door opened, and I walked quickly to Jack's apartment. The doorman let me upstairs. I went inside and poured myself a glass of wine! Shortly after, Jack walked in and said, I left my date to come home to you!

Once again, we were having great conversation and laughing like we were two school kids, the drinks were flowing, and we were having genuine fun. Then, halfway through the night, he received a call from an old friend of ours who said, "I have two available slots on a yacht to the Bahamas, and you guys should come."

Of course, we both said yes. So, we continued the night, and I stayed over. I woke that next morning with a pounding headache and Jack yelling. "We are going to the Bahamas."

I didn't really remember much of the night, and then I realized Holy Shit! We were going to the Bahamas!! I couldn't believe any of that. I hadn't spoken to this man in four years, and the next thing I knew, I was going on a yacht with him for eight days.

We prepared for the trip as it was during COVID, so we needed to obtain all the necessary test results. As we were getting our COVID tests, I looked at Jack and started crying. Not tears of sadness, but tears of happiness. Never in my life would I think I would be going on a private yacht via a private jet to the Bahamas. In some weird way, I felt like I didn't deserve it. Like it was too good to be true. I had that way of thinking only because I was always given the shit end of the stick, so I was in complete shock for something good to happen to me! The excitement between the two of us was overwhelming. Just pure happiness.

At the airport, he looked at me and said, "You know I want to be with you, and I know you aren't ready, but let's just enjoy this trip together."

I agreed, and we were on our way.

We arrived in the Bahamas and were escorted to the yacht. I have never in my life seen anything so beautiful. We adored the people we were with since we had known them for a long time. They were overjoyed for us. They were lovely people who always longed for us to be together. The weather was amazing every day, and the food was unbelievable. We would go from the sundeck to the beach to the jet ski, and there wasn't a worry in the world for any of us. This was something I had never experienced before. I had constantly been worried my whole life, even as a child. So, to not worry for once was such a great feeling for me.

Jack and I had been very close to each other the whole trip. I constantly wanted to be around him, and he wanted the same as well. The crew on the yacht was so pleased to see us together even though they had known us only for a few days.

One day during the trip, the girls went on a beach trip. They kept telling me how much they loved Jack and me together. I instantly asked them to cut out the crap as soon as they started saying such stuff and told them we were only friends.

They all looked at me at one point and said, "He loves you so much, Amanda. You should let your guard down and open your heart to him."

I was still a little pessimistic about the 'relationship' topic, so I told them that it would never work out with Jack. I didn't understand why I couldn't say yes to him. I was saying yes to all these toxic men but refused to be in a relationship with Jack.

I took a few moments to myself and thought hard about why I couldn't say yes to him. The love was there; the passion was there, the chemistry and everything else was there. I thought they might be right about Jack and me a few days later. He was very kind to me; I loved, protected, cherished, and above all, I trusted him. We had a group dinner that evening, and I told one of the crew members that I would ask him to be my boyfriend.

I wasn't worried since I knew Jack had desired this for a long time. So, we created a heart out of shells on a blanket with candles and drinks, and I wrote a message on a piece of paper that said, "Will you be my boyfriend?"

We slightly burned it before putting it in a bottle, like a message you would find washed up on shore. The stars sparkled so brightly in the night sky. I told him I had a surprise for him and brought him down on the lower deck. His eyes lit up with joy when he saw what I had set up for us. We sat together with our wine and then he noticed the bottle with the note in it. He opened the note, and without any hesitation, he said, "YES."

And just like that... Jack and I were in a relationship! We had a wonderful time for the rest of our vacation! Everyone else was overjoyed, knowing that I was finally in a relationship that was worthy of me. We returned to New York City after the most beautiful trip. It was now the end of August which is when my birthday was. I had already had a few plans for a party and was excited for my friends to meet Jack. He was that guy that was very social and outgoing, so my friends adored him within minutes of meeting him.

Everything was going great, we had such a love for each other that nothing could stop us, or so I thought. However, we were a few months into our relationship, and I knew we needed to talk about how to navigate things with his family. His ex-wife had moved on, but they did have children together. We knew our relationship may cause some friction with his family.

He spoke with his children about it, and they understood where Jack was coming from. They all just wanted their dad to be happy, as that is what mattered to them. But we knew it would not be as easy as it seemed. However, I knew that our love for each other, in my opinion, could overcome everything. We were living the good life, having fun, enjoying fantastic get-togethers, traveling, and falling more in love with each other every day. It was so addictive for me since I wanted to be around this man constantly, and he wanted the same. Every time we saw each other, we smiled so much like it was the first time we had met.

I eventually met a few of his children, and they were wonderful. Even though they said that they were all right with their dad being in a relationship with me, I could easily guess that they were not ready to be around me which I totally understood. These types of situations take time for everyone involved. Not all of them were ready, but I did treat them with the utmost respect. I saw Jack as a great dad and wanted to help him and watch the kids succeed in life. I came from a small family, and I adored the way he was with his children. I wanted to be part of that with him in time, obviously. I was not close with his children, but I was trying my best. This was a lot for me. I was never in a situation like this before and was not sure how to navigate it. He wasn't sure either, but we moved forward and tried to do the best we could.

As the months went on, I was feeling very left out. Jack was not the best at communicating with me about what was happening. He would frequently ignore talking about it altogether or would change the topic whenever I brought it up with him.

There weren't many conversations on how we could all fix the situation so everyone could be comfortable. It was more like it was okay for Amanda to be upset. It was upsetting for me, and it made me feel very unwanted. As a child, I felt unwanted at times and never really had a good group of friends or was on a team, so I always felt a bit left out. Unfortunately, I carried that with me in my adult years. I understood me being around would take time, but I just wanted to be heard.

Months passed, and I became increasingly frustrated as if I wasn't wanted in my relationship. I've now become a low priority on his list, and I couldn't understand why. His children should always come first, and I was okay with that; the problem was that everything else also came before me. I tried to be helpful since I knew he was going through a lot, but my feelings were ignored.

This was the beginning of our demise. He was never able to speak with me about what was going on. He rarely told me how the kids were feeling, and if he did, it was concise answers and being annoyed by all my questions. Which I am sure felt like nagging, as I was constantly asking because I didn't know where I stood in any of this.

I realize it takes time, but I thought I needed to be informed. I could see he was becoming unhappy. Our drunken nights turned into fights instead of fun. I started feeling insecure and unhappy. But I always was the one not to give up on relationships that easily and would go all the way to fight tooth and nail for the person I love and my relationship. So, I did. I decided to talk to him about our little messy situation. One night, after we had one of our fights, I told him we needed to talk about it and work together rather than go against each other, he agreed, and things began looking up. He agreed he would make more of an effort to have me involved. It was a good conversation, and I appreciated it as now I at least knew we were going to work together on this.

It was almost Christmas time, and I knew we weren't going to spend the holidays together, which, again, I was fine with as I knew it would take time to become a part of his family to be enjoying the holidays together. We went our separate ways for Christmas that year, but I did put presents under the tree for the kids. I thought that a fresh start would be beneficial for us. After the holidays, we decided that we would move in together as my lease was up. I wasn't sure if I was ready, but we pretty much already spent every day together. I thought, how would living together be any different? We moved into this stunning two-bedroom apartment on the Upper East Side with its own rooftop. We wanted to get two bedrooms so that maybe the kids would feel comfortable coming over and staying.

I was overjoyed to be with him every day, and I know he felt the same way. I decorated the apartment to our needs, made it our own, and ensured the second-floor bedroom was decorated well and had everything it needed for his kids to stay. I was never in a situation where the person I was dating had children, but for some reason, his kids meant the world to me. I wanted so badly to be a part of their life as well in the best possible way. I would message them on birthdays and holidays. I would wish them luck on their exams or their games. I never realized what it was, but my heart was very fond of all of them, and I wanted each of them to succeed in whatever it was they were doing. I didn't want to be some sort of stepmom or anything like that. I just wanted the best for them.

Jack and I moved in, and we couldn't be happier about it. I felt like we were going to be okay. The kids started coming more often to our place and stayed. It felt like it was going to be okay. There was still the hiccup of me not being able to attend their events, but they were comfortable coming over for dinner. It still hurt me deeply, but I was trying my best to hold those feelings in as I felt like I needed to be patient, and it would change. One night we were all snuggled up by our fireplace, and Jack looked at me and said, "I can't wait to spend the rest of my life with you."

I had never felt love as I did for this man before. I truly wanted to start my life with him, but he was still dealing with so much. I wanted to help him and make all his problems disappear, but he didn't want to hear it. I knew our situation was still bothering him as he was all caught up in the middle. I knew he was trying his best to make everyone happy, but he knew he would put me last. We started to get back in that rut again, and I wasn't sure if I could be strong enough to keep fighting for him and us.

We would have drinks when out or at home, and I couldn't handle it. The pain I had inside was so much that I would lash out crying, yelling, and screaming when I would drink. It was like all my emotions came flooding out at once. It was a terrible feeling for him and for me as well.

I felt so unwanted in my relationship. I couldn't understand how he went from absolute admiration for me to nothing. I felt so lost, I felt depressed, I felt unwanted, and I cried a lot. I wasn't doing yoga and going to a very dark place that I had never had in my life before.

It became a serious issue for which I started therapy. I'd never been in anything like this before, and I couldn't handle it any longer. A lot of questions started running down my mind. What did I do wrong that he didn't respect me? Why wasn't I good enough this time?

I was convinced there was something seriously wrong with me. He made me feel like I was the source of our problems. What caused this to happen? What happened to the Jack I used to know and love, who adored and loved me? That guy had vanished.

My therapist was helpful, she was trying to make me see that Jack had issues that he needs to deal with, and his actions are causing me to have bad reactions. She showed me that I had issues that I need to resolve as well. Therapy was actually very helpful, and I asked Jack to join me for one session, but that is something he wasn't ready to do. So, I did it by myself for a few months. I battled for us on my own. He could see I was hurting, so he would do cute date nights or take me on trips, but it wasn't helping. The up and downs were an emotional rollercoaster for me, and I was again lashing out.

He began going out a lot, refusing to return my calls, and arriving home late. I rarely knew where he was and what he was doing. I'd simply sit on our bed and cry, wondering why all of that was happening to me. I would beg Niall to help me. I would ask God to help me. I was beginning to appear insane, and I would call and text him in rage because he ignored me. He would come home and apologize, and I would fall for it, and we just kept continuing. It was like I was numb, though. We would have good times, but then something would happen, and we would get back in our ruts. The good times made me always feel like there was hope and that we would be okay if I kept fighting for us. Again, all of that stemmed from my childhood. I wasn't giving up on this man.

We were still much in love with one other, but the fighting continued. So, we spoke again and promised to work on it. The problem was that I was the only one who was working on it. I couldn't handle it anymore as he continued hurting me. He'd ask me to one of the kid's games, and I'd be overjoyed until the day before, he'd say, "Sorry, you can't go now."

I just wanted to be a tiny part of everything. I didn't want to cause harm. I just wanted everyone to get along. I knew he wanted me to be a part of everything, but he felt that he would upset his children and his ex-wife, so it seemed like it was easier for everyone that I was upset instead.

It had been a year, and he had thrown me the most magnificent birthday party, and I thought to myself, "We got this. Everything will be OKAY!"

It was a wonderful party. All my friends and his friends came, and we were just so happy. Everyone once again loved the way we were with each other. It was mad, to be honest, the love we exuberated was something so addictive, but then in the same breath, we would get into such exhausting arguments.

He surprised me with a trip to Greece for my birthday. Once again, I said to myself okay, we have this. Let's just start over. I had never been to Greece, and what a beautiful place. Laying at the pool overlooking Santorini just made us feel like we were back to the old Jack and Amanda. Jack rented a private boat for the day for us, and we had the most wonderful day together. We were laughing again; we were happy again. We spent the whole week there and had beautiful moments but did end up having an argument one night. After that, it started to get exhausting for both of us.

I kept fighting and supporting him because I believed he was going through a lot. I knew he was hurting as well. I knew I was the only person in his life that he could take his anger out on and still be there to support him, but I was losing myself, and it was catching up with me because I put him first. I was in excruciating pain and couldn't take it anymore.

I kept my feelings to myself, and we kept on going once again. My mind was always racing with ideas, and I was frightened about him. He stood to lose everything, and I didn't want that for him. We had a bad argument in October before he departed for a Chicago trip. The next morning, he called me and told me it was over. I was devastated when he broke up with me over the phone.

The worst sensation wasn't even devastation. My heart had been broken. I was completely shattered. Kiki talked me down from the ledge when I phoned him, distraught and in tears, but I wasn't listening. How could he end everything over the phone? If anyone should have ended it, it should have been me. I had been there for him for years, battled tirelessly for us, stayed up late at night making sure he got home safely, and always treated him and his children with nothing but respect. I phoned my mom, distraught, unable to catch my breath, and she just told me to come home. I was texting him, pleading with him not to do it. I booked a ticket home and spent a few days there.

I called him every day, crying, and told him we could fix it. I couldn't do anything except for cry for the following few days. I just stayed at my mom's place and kept telling him to please not do this. I had to return to New York City to confront him, as we were still living together at the time. I returned to the apartment, where he instantly approached me, began crying, and gave me the biggest hug. From that, I got the impression that maybe he did really want our relationship to work out. He simply looked at me and apologized and walked away from me.

We went back and forth for days, and every time I would cry and talk about us trying to work things out, he would transform into a man I had never seen before. It was as if I didn't matter to him. He didn't want to talk about it and didn't seem to mind that I was sobbing on the floor. It made things worse for me when he turned into a cold person. How did all of this come to be? How could he treat me so badly? I couldn't handle the pain. Of course, I had my mom and friends to comfort me, but I just couldn't handle it.

One night as I was upstairs, he told me he was thinking about moving to Florida, even though our lease wasn't up for another five months. He just broke up with me, and now he was going to move to another state! It made no sense because he was so close to his children that there was no way he would move to another state. This just infuriated me and made things so much worse. Nothing made sense, and I felt like something was going on that I didn't know about. This man was making me crazy, and mentally, I was unstable. I made up many scenarios in my head of what was happening.

I needed to find a place to live. I wasn't ready to move out financially, and my credit wasn't great. I walked the streets every day seeking anything and was becoming upset because I needed to get out of there. I lost everything in a week and had no control over it. I lost my boyfriend, best friend, and the place that I had called my home. It had all vanished without me having any say. I felt like the day when I was let go from my job when I arrived in New York City, everything was gone in a blink of an eye and was out of my control.

I knew we were frequently arguing, but I honestly believed that everything would be alright if we both worked together. He would tell me how much he loved me and how sorry he was but in such a cold tone. Eventually, I found an apartment and moved out. I knew I needed to get away from him. After about a month, we contacted each other about the apartment as it was in both of our names. He claimed he had leased it and was relocating to Florida, which I rolled my eyes at. I was relieved, though. The apartment was gone, so we didn't have to keep upkeep on that.

I was still crying every day, taking Nyquil at night to sleep, and staring at my phone every day, hoping for him to call, waiting for a text to say, "let's fix this." But none of those ever happened. As a result, I fell into a deep depression. How could he do such a thing to me? He proclaims his love for me from the highest peaks and then abandons me. I needed to talk to him, so we met for dinner one night, and he cried and apologized for being so cruel to me the whole time because he believed it would be easier for me to go if he was a jerk, which only added more pain to my misery. After dinner that night, I thought maybe we could at least be cordial.

I took him out on his birthday the following week since I didn't want him to be alone on his special day. I know you are all thinking, 'Amanda, you're an idiot. You're taking this man out for his birthday after he broke your heart?'

Once again, my big heart got me in trouble, and I still had some sort of hope. That night, we ended up drinking, and he continued telling me how much he loved me and how much he still wanted me in his life. Which really messed me up emotionally. We spent that night together. He left early the next morning then it was back to like I didn't even exist, which made things so much worse for me.

Every day, I would chat with my mom and my girlfriends for hours, and they helped me get through it. I had been a strong person, yet I was so weak to this man. I did block him at one point, but I didn't keep it up. It was getting close to Christmas, and he was messaging me a lot, apologizing, and wishing me a happy holiday, and that's when I got COVID. As a result, I was unable to travel home for the holidays and was forced to stay in my apartment alone to deal with the pain. To have to sit alone and deal with such pain was something I would never wish upon anyone.

He called one night, expressed his desire to see me, and asked if we might have brunch together when he was in town. So, of course, I couldn't say no. That day, I met him, and we had the loveliest time. He hugged me tightly as soon as he saw me and told me how much he missed me and how pleased he was to see me. Every time I walked into a room, and he saw me, he would immediately smile, and his eyes would light up, which always warmed my heart. He apologized to me several times more and expressed his feelings and love for me.

It felt like back in the day when we had so much fun together! Just really enjoying each other. During our conversation, he told me that he was using a dating app. I mean, is this guy serious? He was sitting right across from me, telling me he loved me and then telling me that he was using a dating app in the same breath. I got upset about it, but Jack was always good at talking his way out of situations, and he did it again. And the emotional fool I sometimes get to be, I believed him. Once again, we had a great night, and I went away feeling like maybe there was hope. In some weird way, I still knew he loved me deeply, and the way he had treated me wasn't who he was as a person deep down in his heart.

He went back to Florida, and we were constantly chatting. He even asked me to come to visit him there. Red flags were everywhere, and I ignored them all. This guy broke my heart, and I was like, oh, fun! I'll come anyways.

As a result, I said yes. He was so loving to me before I came to Florida and really made me feel desired. When I arrived in Florida, he picked me up from the airport. When I walked out and saw him, I wanted to cry with happiness. The smile on his face was from ear to ear, like the time we met at the bar on the Hudson River.

He hugged me tightly. He continued expressing his happiness that I was there. We arrived at his apartment and immediately headed to the beach with some wine. I felt great as he was telling his neighbors I was his girl! I thought, "Maybe we can get through this."

That day was fantastic, and the night was even better. We pretended to be back together again. He was holding my hand, cuddling with me, and being romantic with me. I felt fantastic! This was the man I always fought for.

We were drinking halfway through the week when he told me that he had been on a dates with another women. Jack was an open book when he was drinking and had no filter, so he would tell me everything. Tears started to well up in my eyes, but I knew I had to stay strong. I couldn't believe he was going on dates! It had only been three months since we broke up. God knows what he had been doing all this time. But I disregarded it since I knew it would spoil my week, and I wanted to enjoy myself. We spent the rest of the week together as if we had never been apart.

We traveled together to New York City at the end of the week. We got to the airport, and with tears in my eyes, I told him I would never see him again. I knew I had to get away from this man. I knew he would hurt me again.

He looked at me and said, "I understand, and you are right."

We landed in LaGuardia, and at baggage claim, he hugged me. That was the last time I saw Jack. My heart was shattered into so many pieces. I truly did love that man. Deep down in his heart, I knew he loved me too, but in the end, it just wasn't enough.

I had a lot of bad days after this, and I had some good days. I always wondered, on days that were clearer than the rest, maybe I was Jack's living angel. Maybe I was put in his life for him to find some happiness and put a smile on his face. Maybe I was there to show him that you can't find happiness in another person. You must be happy with yourself first; that person will be a great addition to your life. I also knew that he was just going through a lot which really didn't have to deal with how he felt for me. He just didn't know how to deal with all of it. They always say, "hurt people, hurt people," which I do believe. We were both hurting and didn't know how to filter and acknowledge each other's feelings. I knew his situation was tough, and the timing was all wrong for us to be in a relationship. I knew in my heart what he did was not intentional. He was trying so hard to make everyone happy that he lost himself. He lost that guy you all read about in the beginning. I know I did make him happy at times, and I am still grateful because that is all I ever wanted.

In the end, it was an experience for sure, and I knew it was finally the end of Jack and Amanda... or was it?

CHAPTER 10

DIFFICULT ROADS, LEAD TO BEAUTIFUL PLACES

It is now a full twelve years from the day I moved to New York City. I'm watching everyone pass by as I sit in my local coffee shop and am curious about their New York City experiences. I wrote this book because I wanted others to be able to connect to some of the experiences I had. The experiences that I have written about are true, but I do leave some details out as I don't want to hurt anyone's feelings. I wanted everyone to read this and realize that suffering does not persist indefinitely. For the longest time here, I've been asking myself, "Why me? What did I do to go through all this suffering? Why was I continually receiving the short end of the stick, especially in relationships, when I felt like I always did the right thing by people?"

During my twelve years in New York City, I was very hard on myself, and there were many instances in my life when I thought I wasn't good enough. The relationships I was in really did take a toll on me.

I always wondered, did these men know they were hurting me? Did they understand they were making me sad? Did they say sorry to make it all go away for them? To me, the answer had always been a big NO. They would say sorry to me, but they had no idea what they were apologizing for. They had no idea the pain I was going through during and after. I truly believed they didn't even want to understand my feelings. I've always been a confident person, but when people you care about manage to make you feel like you are not good enough, it hurts.

I got depressed and became insecure. I became so many things that weren't even me. I always wanted to feel wanted by others for some reason, and when I didn't get that, I felt like all the good that I did do for them was just nothing. I felt empty inside. I desperately wanted to get back to that Amanda I once knew, the one with the glow about her and the smile on her face.

I know more than a few of these chapters are about the failed relationships and how I was hurt, but I also made many mistakes as well and lashed out at times in those situations. No one is perfect, and everyone makes mistakes. We can't change what has happened to us in the past, that is gone, but we can change how we act in the present day and in our future. Being in those relationships and those situations made me realize what I deserved, but why couldn't I mentally grasp it then?

I felt back then that the chaos was normal, and the bad behavior on both sides was normal. That is why I would leave one bad relationship and go straight into another one. Of course, I wrote about the bad moments because I wanted to help people overcome the tough times. But, of course, there were great moments in all the relationships you read about. This isn't a book about ruining all my exes' lives or creating any sort of problem for them, it's a book to help, and maybe this helps them understand people's feelings and acknowledge them in future situations. We will all face difficulties, but our experiences shape who we are. It's during these times we figure out how to be better or how to help someone else.

As you read, death and relationships caused a lot of my misery. As I wrote this book and re-read through it one hundred times, I saw a very sad Amanda. At the time, I knew I was sad but didn't realize how bad it was. I always held my feelings in and walked around with a smile on my face, which made things so much worse. I didn't realize this until I went to therapy.

For most chapters, I was crying and going through a traumatic experience, but as I look back, I know that those experiences are what made me who I am today. Never would I think I was going to be okay all those years ago. Never would I think I would have a great career, a lovely apartment, and more knowledge of life and relationships. I think it takes all these lessons to help you understand yourself better. All of this felt so terrible at the time. I will say that, but it made me respect myself so much more. It took letting go to realize I was holding on to nothing in each of those experiences.

I vowed to myself this New Year that I would write a book. I also stated that I would do more for Amanda. It's okay to say no to people and to be selfish every now and again. Saying no was something I rarely did because I was always afraid that if I said no, to that person, it would upset them, and they would leave me. Now I understand that it is okay, and if that person does leave, then that is something they must deal with on their end. I have learned that my big heart isn't a curse. Those people just couldn't grasp it, which is okay.

Self-care is vital, and we all deserve it. We need to be a bit selfish, and we also need to be thankful. We need to thank ourselves for everything. We need to thank others who are in our lives and support us. We need love, we need support, and we need to feel wanted. Thanking people is something so easy, and I feel like we rarely do it. Of course, we say thank you to someone who opens the door or takes your order at a restaurant, but I am talking about a real thank you. Reach out to someone and really say thank you for who they are in your life. It can really make someone's day.

I also think change is important. I feel like I have changed a good bit since then. When people read the word change, they instantly get afraid and persist in not changing themselves. They would rather say, "I am who I am, and I just like it that way."

When I say change, I don't mean change entirely, but I feel like we need to change some things regarding how we act. Again, not one of us is perfect, so there are some tweaks we need to make in life. One of my changes and I am continually working on it, is not to react to other people's actions. If that is how that person wants to treat me, I just say okay and acknowledge their behavior and try not to get upset about it. It's not me, it's them, and I must realize that. I have and am still practicing how to acknowledge my mistakes and take accountability for them. I am also working on not "fixing" everyone. I have learned the hard way that if someone wants help, they will ask for it.

Life can be tough, and we really need to do the work to ensure we treat people correctly. I don't want anyone to be hurt because I know being hurt isn't great. Will we trip in life? Absolutely! But it's a practice, and that is all we can do.

I continue to practice yoga every week, and it helps me keep going. It gave me the ability to live in the present moment. You can't alter the past, and you can't foresee the future. So, let's not be concerned about it. It took me twelve years, two deaths, and a handful of poor relationships to comprehend that phrase. I would never want any of you reading this to go through that, but as the title of this chapter reads, "difficult roads lead to beautiful places," I truly believe that.

It's difficult to remain optimistic because our ego takes control of our minds and fills our thoughts with negative ones. Yoga taught me that feeding your ego will lead you down the wrong path. It will completely consume you. So once again, we need to try our hardest not to feed those negative thoughts. Believe me, I know I am preaching to the choir here. I let my ego take over my mind for twelve years, probably longer, and it still does. So, I must keep on practicing acknowledging when it does happen.

Through this process, I also tried to acknowledge how to forgive others. I come from a family where if someone disrespects you, that is it, do not forgive them, and never speak to them again. For a long time, I felt like that made sense. I now see-through yoga and other mental health practices that we do need to forgive. We need to forgive because the person that hurt us might also be hurting. We need to hold peace in our hearts as that will allow positive things to happen to us. Do you forget what that person did? No. You acknowledge their actions and move on. I can't hold people responsible for their flaws. I can only be responsible for my actions. We must continue to progress and do good in the world. So many people are in pain and try to disguise it, leading to them doing stupid things. I'll raise my hand right away. Nobody understands everyone's story or how they are feeling. That is why we must be kind to everyone, as we have no idea what they are going through.

What occurred to me shaped me into the person I am today. It helped me understand how strong I am and how I can overcome any obstacle. I put forth a lot of effort; I went through a lot of pain and heartbreak, but it didn't kill me. With that stated, I understand this is not the conclusion of my story. I am aware that I will continue to face challenges throughout my life. We'll all do. All you must do is see how to deal with hardships and what you can learn from them.

I'm not sure what the next several years will bring for me. Will I ever marry? Will I ever have children? Will I switch jobs? Will I remain in New York City? Will Jack ever text me at random? Will I ever see James again? Will I be living an entirely different life that I am unaware of? Who knows! And I'm okay with not worrying about it. I'm fine with living in the now and savoring every moment of it.

Maybe some of you, after you read this, will say, "I went through the same things as she did." I must tell you that you will be okay. You will be fine, but you must put in the effort. Find something you like and are enthusiastic about and admit when you make a mistake.

Recognize your mistakes and be grateful for what you have, even if it isn't where you want to be at the time. Find something to be thankful for and express gratitude to yourself. Thank yourself for being courageous and trying your best.

We live in such a harsh environment these days, and it is challenging to be a good person. I guarantee you'll be satisfied if you put in the effort. You'll be in good hands. It's also fine to be a little selfish. Make time for yourself. Getting to that beautiful place is not simple, but it's doable. The stories I just told are only the tip of the iceberg in terms of my life. We all have problems, but we need to do our best to recognize them, so then we will be guided to the path that is meant for us. We all have a journey, and if we stay positive, we will be guided to the one we deserve. In the end, I hope my story can be someone else's survival guide.

ACKNOWLEDGMENTS

I didn't want to end on that note, so I will end with how thankful I am for everyone that has been in my life during my New York City experiences. I feel like this is the speech you give at the Emmys, and it is so long that they start playing the music to cut you off.

To my Mom, thank you for letting me move to a city at a young age with no money. This woman was there for me every step of the way during all these experiences you just read about and obviously more throughout my life. She was there even when I did stupid things and made horrible mistakes. She was there to answer the phone daily while I went through each struggle; there for me with no judgment. She knew I would figure it out but also knew how to be supportive. So, thank you, Mom, for always being my rock and my best friend. I love you.

To Sarah, thank you for helping me through my first few months of arriving in New York City. I had no clue what I was doing and had litte money. This girl walked me through every step of a terrifying new journey. She also knew I could do anything I put my mind to, even if I didn't listen to her. She pushed me to take this journey regardless of what would happen.

To my Brooklyn Boys, I will always look at you both as big brothers and appreciate you making me feel safe and protected living with you all in Brooklyn. I appreciate your effort in making me feel like we were a small family.

To Connor, thank you for giving me a job after I felt like my life was over, for introducing me to Niall and, to this day, my very best friends Tony and Phillip and other friends. The pub will always be my first home in New York City and will always hold a special place in my heart. Letting me be a part of your family when I had no one will be forever grateful.

To Gemma, thank you for being my ride-or-die homegirl always. For always having my back, always being my voice of reason, and always buying an obscene amount of nonsense at the Rite Aid after a night of drinking.

To James, thank you for showing me I am a fighter and my compassion for people is good. Also, showing me

London to which I now have such an obsession with, and showing me that it is okay to fight for what I want.

To Kiki, Cici, Anthony, and Gigi, thank you for keeping me sane after so many traumatic situations. These men have been there for me every second of every day to support me through my hardest and darkest days and nights. There was never a moment they didn't answer or give me sound advice, especially Kiki. Our friendship means the world to me. I knew at any time I could call him, and he would either calm me down or explain to me that I couldn't keep doing this to myself. He watched me suffer terribly and supported me with care and love. He let me go through the process, though, he knew I needed to hurt, and I needed to suffer to be able to come out on the other side. Very grateful for them all.

To the Doc, thank you for being my New York City mom. You took a chance on a broken girl who didn't know much about where she was in life or where she was going. You took a chance on a defeated girl, and I knew the day I interviewed you saw that in my eyes. You saw that I was about to leave New York City and come to the terms that I had failed. Thank you for taking me in as one of your own at work and in your personal life. I truly am grateful to you.

To Jack, a lot of this book is about him, and he was in my life for a very long time. I can start with he never let me make an excuse to do anything short of being the best in my career. If it wasn't for him, I wouldn't have taken those exams and progressed in my career. Next, I thank him for making me feel loved at multiple points in our relationship, regardless of the bad times. The moments that he made me feel loved were so special to me. I am thankful for the times he looked at me as if no one else was in the room and the times he protected me. Our love will always be something that I will cherish. I am grateful that I was able to experience it. I will never forget those moments and always have an enormous amount of love for him, so thank you, Jack.

Lastly, I would like to thank ME. Thank me for being strong, thank me for crying, thank me for making mistakes, thank me for being vulnerable. Thank me for not giving up on my dream; even when I found myself at such lows, that failure would have been so much easier. This may seem silly to some, but we need to thank ourselves sometimes for the hard work we do and continue to do. I can thank so many others, but I think this is where the music starts, and I get kicked off the stage.

As I mentioned earlier, I have no clue what my future holds. I guess we will just have to wait until book number two comes out.

DEDICATION

I am sure many of you are wondering why the dedication is at the end of the book. I wanted you all to first read about Niall and who he was as a person and our what our friendship was.

This book is dedicated to Niall Gibbons, my New York City Angel. To the man who supported me every day on my journey. You were put in my life as my angel, and that was one of your many jobs. You were put here to guide me through my struggles and hardships. I will be forever grateful for that. I will be forever grateful for our friendship. I love you with all my heart and soul and always will. I will always have this book and so will you.

www.ingramcontent.com/pod-product-compliance
Lightning Source LLC
Chambersburg PA
CBHW050742230626
47052CB00004BA/1037